# KERRICK

## The Mavericks, Book 01

# Dale Mayer

KERRICK: THE MAVERICKS, BOOK 1
Beverly Dale Mayer
Valley Publishing Ltd.

Copyright © 2019



ISBN-13: 978-1-773361-99-4
Print Edition

# About This Book

What happens when the very men—trained to make the hard decisions—come up against the rules and regulations that hold them back from doing what needs to be done? They either stay and work within the constraints given to them or they walk away. Only now, for a select few, they have another option:

The Mavericks. A covert black ops team that steps up and break all the rules … but gets the job done.

Welcome to a new military romance series by *USA Today* best-selling author Dale Mayer. A series where you meet new friends in this raw and compelling look at the men who keep us safe every day from the darkness where they operate—and live—in the shadows … until someone special helps them step into the light.

**On the precipice of change … Just not the way he'd expected …**

Kerrick is tagged to join a new elite group, where he'd have more say and less rules on missions. Working mostly alone, he's to track down a kidnapped victim suspected of being in England, and likely she's not the only one. This is his kind of job; finding out a longtime friend is his backup makes this mission a go.

Amanda is snatched at the end of her workday while walking to her vehicle. Days later she wakes to find she's imprisoned, alone in a small cement cell. One rotting meal a day is provided, and that is it. Once she realizes someone else is here–a young boy—she's even more determined to escape. And to take him with her. Running into Kerrick wasn't the plan …

Escaping is only one part of the puzzle as the truth drags them to Europe and beyond as they sort out how the two kidnappings are related, who's behind it all and why … Before they are run aground and imprisoned all over again …

**Sign up to be notified of all Dale's releases here!**
https://geni.us/DaleNews

# Books in This Series

Kerrick, Book 1

Griffin, Book 2

Jax, Book 3

Beau, Book 4

Asher, Book 5

Ryker, Book 6

Miles, Book 7

Nico, Book 8

Keane, Book 9

Lennox, Book 10

Gavin, Book 11

Shane, Book 12

Diesel, Book 13

Jerricho, Book 14

Killian, Book 15

Hatch, Book 16

Corbin, Book 17

Aiden, Book 18

Boxed Sets and Bundles

https://geni.us/Bundlepage

# CHAPTER 1

KERRICK CASSIDY LOOKED at the text message and frowned.

**Meet at 1830.**

He knew who the sender was, but he hadn't heard from this guy in a long time. He had always been a bit on the raw side, a law unto himself, a maverick among humans. Kerrick had heard he'd gone into the military but had lost track of him. Was it the same friend? Kerrick's phone ID'd the man's name and number. Or rather, a version of his nickname.

Kerrick sent a quick message back. **Where and why?**

**Waterside Pub.** That pub—or dive—was just inside the San Diego city limits but still close to where Kerrick now stood in his apartment in Coronado. Waterside was more of a locals' hangout, and one Kerrick knew well. As he thought about it, he realized it's where he'd met this friend a long time ago. But there was no explanation as to the *why* part of the message. At that, he frowned, checking his watch. It was 5:35 p.m. now. He had no plans. He had enough time to make the meeting, even with Friday night traffic.

So, was that a coincidence, or was something else going on here? He sent his old friend an affirmative reply while standing and staring out the window of his small apartment. He was living on the Coronado base in standard base housing, but that was short-term. As in, very short-term.

Like, … his entire military career was soon over. He was done with the navy. At least in the capacity he'd served.

He was at a crossroads in his life, one that he looked forward to but, at the same time, he'd given a lot of his best years to the navy. He'd been part of their elite group, but sometimes the people around you changed, and the people above you changed, and Kerrick had been chafing at the rules and the regulations for a long time. He was one of the more senior guys and knew that he should be moving on. Others had gone on to have life partners and families, rounding out their lives. Kerrick didn't have either of those things to keep him grounded.

He used to, but that was a long time ago. He and his wife had been childhood sweethearts. He'd only been in the navy a couple years and hadn't even made it to his elite group yet when she and their six-month-old daughter had been killed in a car accident. Some men hit the bottle; others managed to recover from life-changing events like that. In his case, Kerrick locked all the hurt inside and had faced the world, angrier, harder, and more determined to bury himself and all his pain in his work.

Kerrick stared at his phone, frowning, wondering if he should show up for this meet. He didn't have any reason not to. The thing was, the longer he'd been in the service, the more Kerrick understood other men's struggles with the regimented lifestyle. While Kerrick had taken solace in the rules and regulations, others had chafed at the restrictions. Kerrick had more of a get-along-with and do-the-job type of attitude. He'd been all about the team.

As the teams had expanded, and as the number of members in this elite group had totaled several thousand, the atmosphere had changed. It was great if you could stay in the group that you loved and with the men who you knew and trusted. But, when they left or were transferred, it became an ever-changing sea of faces. The status was changing too, and he wasn't sure he wanted to have unknown guys, untested guys, guys ten years younger than him watching his back.

And he knew that they looked at him and worried that maybe Kerrick was past his prime. Just the thought of that angered him. No way he was washed-up. Not at thirty-four. But something was definitely different in his outlook now. And it went beyond the everlasting agony of losing his wife and child. It was another kind of ache in his soul. He wanted to do more; he wanted to go into foreign countries and take out the insurgents like they needed to be taken out.

But he was forever being held back by the politically correct actions as dictated by the brass above. And sometimes it really chafed to have men a long ways away make decisions about matters they couldn't possibly comprehend, not without boots on the ground. Hell, even friendly fire was an issue on the bases. If the brass couldn't handle the fights in their own bases, how were they deemed worthy to supervise any op in a foreign country?

He shook his head, grabbed his keys, and walked out. He locked the door behind him, feeling a sense of finality in the movement. Although he slept here, he didn't really live here. He kept his civilian clothes to a minimum. He was always ready to leave at a moment's notice, and he cared about nothing in that place. The memories of his wife and daughter were the only things that still mattered, and he kept those inside. Sure, he'd had relationships since losing them, but those quick hookups had been more for him to reconnect to the world and maybe to let off some steam and just to have a bit of fun every once in a while. His heart, however, was well-guarded.

Nobody walked away from an experience like his without some scars to show for it. And he had yet to find a way to manage those scars. And the physical scars on his body? Well, he didn't give a crap about those. They were beyond fixing and were so much a part of him that even he'd forgotten how he'd gotten a lot of them. And none of them bothered him, yet he knew it would bother other women. Not the females he tended to spend time with now. They couldn't care less. They just wanted a good hard ride, and he was up for that any day.

But the softer side of a real relationship—with love, true love, like that special relationship he'd had with Aurora—that part he kept hidden. He was afraid his ability to give true love had died permanently with her but held out hope that one day he'd find himself responding emotionally to another woman.

When he walked into the pub five minutes early, he didn't recognize anybody in the smoke-filled room. He ordered a draft off the bar and took it outside. He always preferred to be outside anyway. He found his friend sitting there, in the far corner on the patio, waiting for him and watching him approach. Kerrick studied him as he sat down. "The years haven't been kind," Kerrick said bluntly.

His friend smiled, shook his head, and said, "No, they haven't been. Doesn't look like they've been too kind to you either."

Kerrick shrugged, still bristling at the idea that he might be past his prime, and said, "I'm doing fine."

His friend nodded, and Kerrick stared at him.

"What name are you going by these days?" Kerrick asked.

His friend just smiled and said, "Call me Beta."

Kerrick's eyebrows rose. "As in, second in command, with a leader called *Alpha* above you?"

Beta chuckled and said, "There is a ladder. But I didn't tell you that."

"Sounds like you're still a bit of a maverick." Kerrick crossed his arms, not willing to give an inch to the man trying to read him intently. "Why am I here?"

"Maverick?" Beta rolled the word around on the tip of his tongue and smiled. "I like that. We can use that. Now as to why you are here – answer that question yourself. Why *are* you here?"

Kerrick frowned. Because, of course, that was exactly what he needed to know too. "Curiosity," he said. "Trying to figure out the voice from the past."

"Heard you were having some trouble."

"Not really," Kerrick said, reaching for his beer. He lifted it and sipped but never took his gaze off the man across him. "Just an interesting stage of life. Nothing I can't handle though."

"Do you care to handle it any longer?" Beta asked, leaning forward to study his buddy's eyes.

"Not sure what that means," Kerrick said in a calm tone. "Have you got a job for me? Because I'm no mercenary."

A grin flashed, Beta's white teeth lighting up the evening settling around them. It should have been a hot and sunny day in California, but, with overcast clouds, it wasn't. A storm threatened on the horizon, adding an electric crackle to the air around them. Just the kind of weather that matched Kerrick's mood.

"It would be government-sanctioned," Beta said. "Black ops. Small teams on the ground. Mostly two working alone."

Kerrick felt the shock waves rock through him. "You do know what I have been doing for the last decade, right?"

Beta nodded. "One of the topmost decorated Navy SEAL officers. I'm really proud of you."

"Why?" Kerrick asked. "I never did quite understand the thing about getting medals for doing your damn job."

Beta cracked a smile again. "Still the same old Kerrick. You have a set of honorable rules to live by that few men can match," he said, leaning back casually as he picked up his own beer and drank.

Kerrick nodded. "Definitely have my own set of standards and my own honor system, and I'm loyal. Which is why I can't ever do anything of a mercenary nature."

"It's got nothing to do with that," Beta said calmly. "But I need to know if your heart's still with the Navy SEALs or if you're ready to take a step into something … different."

"How different?"

Beta chuckled. "Maybe not very different at all. We're talking two-man undercover missions, possibly larger teams as we recruit a few more men."

"Who's leading?"

"I am, from a distance," Beta said. "But essentially you're on your own."

In spite of himself, Kerrick could feel the interest surging through him. He leaned forward, his hands gripping the tall beer glass. "How alone? For how long?"

"Only what you feel you need. You're the boss of *your* mission."

Kerrick's eyebrows shot up. "Money?"

"Are you asking about money for your bank account or money available to do what's needed to be done?"

"Both."

"Got you covered. And more."

At that sock to his gut, Kerrick stared at his friend. "How black ops?"

"It doesn't get any darker than this."

"Is this a brand-new US government department? Do we have a code name?"

"Definitely." He grinned. "I just named it The Mavericks."

Kerrick snorted at that. "So, no systems in place. You don't know how it'll work yet?"

"You'd be one of the first to implement it."

"Even if I go in alone," he said, "I still need some people to call on. I need intel. I need maybe a specialist here and there."

Beta nodded. "And you will have backup, of course."

Kerrick frowned at him. "Depends on who the backups are reporting to."

A startled laugh erupted from Beta's lips. "Yeah, the same old Kerrick. Always wanting to know who'll report to whom and who's over your head."

"I want to make sure that nobody is reporting behind my back," Kerrick said. "I want my people loyal to me, to the program, and to whoever is cutting our paychecks. But most of all, loyal to me while on a mission."

"Understood."

But Beta didn't say anything else, so Kerrick wasn't exactly sure just how much leeway he would have. He probed gently. "Budget?"

"Yes."

"How big?"

"More than you can spend in this lifetime," Beta said. And this time, there was no smile. He had settled in, just waiting to see what questions Kerrick would ask.

"I can have anything I need? Do you have the resources?"

"Interesting question."

"Up until now I just walked into the armory and signed out what I needed."

Beta's smile still did not show up. He continued to stare at Kerrick steadily.

"Meaning, I can use my own suppliers?" Kerrick asked to clarify Beta's silence.

Beta gave a shrug. "Nobody—and I mean *nobody*—in the military gets to know about this."

"So, not the usual sources," Kerrick said as he stared out into the landscape. "What about using civilians?"

"No details ever to be given."

"Some of the civilians I know," he said, "don't need to ask questions to understand what's going on."

"Exactly. And, considering it's your cover, and your ass, you might want to watch who you talk to."

Kerrick had a few more questions, but it was kind of hard to sort out details when he didn't know enough about his new employer or about what was expected from him to begin with. Typical government attitude. The navy trained them to obey and to not question. No matter how idiotic the order. And Kerrick had had more than a few of those. Luckily he had lived to complain about them. He understood that some of those follow-orders-without-thinking reflexes may be necessary when fighting a war, but, even then, Kerrick had to think there were other—and better— ways to do things. "Time frame?"

"Are you packed?"

"Always." Kerrick gave a decisive nod, sucked in his

breath, and settled back against his chair. He rapped his fingers on the table, waiting for Beta to say more. To say anything.

Beta smiled and said, "Then get some sleep. It's only chatter now. We're following a person of interest and need more people lined up anyway. We'll call you sometime in the next couple days."

Behind him, a glass shattered on the concrete patio floor. Kerrick shifted to take a look. And, when he turned back, his friend had vaulted over the small porch railing, letting Kerrick catch a glimpse of Beta just as he disappeared around the corner of the building.

Kerrick sat here for a long moment, wondering what the hell he had just got himself into.

# CHAPTER 2

J UST SHY OF forty hours later, at 10:25 a.m. on Sunday, Kerrick got a phone call. Out of the blue, a strange robotic voice on the other end said, "It's time," and promptly hung up.

Ten minutes later Kerrick took a deep breath and stepped outside. No personal belongings were left here. He was no longer part of the Navy SEALs and was moving out of his austere base housing, even though the rent was paid through to the end of the month. But he doubted he would ever be back here to the base again. So, he'd taken care of business first. He didn't say goodbye to anybody because he didn't know if he would see them again and because he could see them one week later. For all he knew, this was a one-time job and nothing else. At the pub, he parked, walked inside, ordered a coffee, and headed out to the same table as before, where he found Beta waiting for him again.

Beta held a brown 9x13 envelope, gave it to him, and said, "You have just about enough time to drink that."

Kerrick nodded, checked his watch—10:58 a.m.—took a long healthy swallow of his black coffee, and then asked, "Where am I going?"

"First job's easy. You're off to England."

Kerrick smiled. "That's almost like staying at home."

"Not necessarily in this case," Beta said. "Take care of

the job, and we'll talk afterward."

And, just like that, he got up, walked back into the pub, and disappeared. Sitting outside alone, Kerrick swiftly emptied the folder and studied its contents. There was a photo of a beautiful young woman's face, her name noted as Dr. Amanda Berg. He frowned at that, her name rattling somewhere around in the back of his brain.

He quickly read her dossier, which stated she was a bio-chemist and had been kidnapped outside a specialized center in France. Their intel said she was somewhere in England, having been seen at the Dover ferry crossing. He frowned again. If she'd been sighted, somebody must have already been following her, and they shouldn't have lost her once she had reached the English shores. He couldn't wait to hear that explanation.

He found plane tickets between the papers. Checking his flight info, leaving at 11:24 a.m., didn't give him any time to finish his coffee. But, after a twelve-and-a-half-hour flight, involving one stop, he should be in London. He stuffed the rest of the file back in the envelope and headed to his vehicle. As he got to the parking lot, a cab waited for him, and his vehicle was nowhere to be found.

The cab driver looked at him and said, "Are you the guy going to the airport on an express run?"

Kerrick asked, "Do you have my bags?"

The cabbie nodded and pointed at a black carry-on duf-fel bag and a small backpack visible on the floorboard of the car.

"Good enough," Kerrick said, already in the back seat. As the cabbie pulled out of the parking lot and headed toward the airport, in the back of his mind, Kerrick won-dered what had happened to his car—which wasn't worth a hell of a lot but was still his. In the taxi, he had just enough time to flip through the rest of the paperwork but not enough time to ingest it all. Just when he thought he'd gone through all the information though, he noticed a tiny microdot in the bottom of the envelope. He pulled it out slowly, staring at it.

Just then the cabbie called out, "Forgot to give you this," and tossed him a box.

In the back of the cab, almost at the airport, he quickly dismantled all the packaging. He took out a pair of sunglasses. A quick inspection didn't reveal anything special about them. Also he found a Bluetooth headpiece that went to the accompanying burner phone. One number had been programmed in.

As soon as he exited the cab at the airport, he walked to the counter and checked in, wondering why he was flying commercial to begin with. Once he was at his gate, he headed into an isolated corner. There, he dialed the one number programmed in his disposable cell. Instead of hearing a voice, a series of tumblers clicked into place. *A secure line. Interesting.*

"State your name."

"Kerrick."

"Full name."

He rolled his eyes and gave it.

"We have you at the airport right now," the voice said. "You will arrive on target according to our schedule."

"Yes, according to the current airport schedule."

"The microdot has information you need," the voice said, "use the sunglasses."

*Hmm. The sunglasses can send info to me? On the lenses themselves, I presume. Interesting.*

"We'll contact you when you land."

He shut off the phone, tucked it in his pocket, and wondered about the cell phone. Depending on how dangerous this op turned out to be, this disposable cell would be one of the first things he dumped. But he couldn't do it yet. He looked at the microdot and sunglasses, finding a small hole to drop in the dot. Then he put on the glasses and stared out the window. Immediately information flowed on the glass lenses, displaying further details on the case. He didn't know what anybody's involvement in this kidnapping was yet. Including his own. If he hadn't known Beta, Kerrick wouldn't have taken this step at all. Beta already knew about Kerrick's history and knew where he was at in this stage of his life. But then, of course, Kerrick had been targeted just for that reason.

DR. AMANDA BERG shifted uncomfortably on the hard bed. It wasn't concrete but it was more like an old metal cot with a mattress on top. Or what had been a mattress at one point in time. It was so thin and so flat that no cushion was left to it. In addition, she only had a thin blanket for warmth. Her initial panic over being kidnapped and drugged had subsided somewhat, and her brain was now finally working again.

She'd been taken off the street right outside the building where she worked, in broad daylight, a hood pulled over her head before being tossed into the back of a lorry, and then locked up in this windowless hellhole. The only glimmer of light that she saw came from outside her solid wood door. All had been a nightmare of silence and fear, but her anger simmered deep beneath the surface.

Was this because of her research work? She came from a wealthy family, but did these kidnappers know that? That didn't matter to her as much as her research. She was working on specific cancer genes and cures too, but did her kidnappers care about that? Not likely. The only person she knew, who hated her, was her ex-husband. Their nasty divorce was still fresh on her mind, even five years later. Probably more on his mind than hers though. She'd figured that she was safe when the ink was finally drying on the legal document, but was she? Was he behind this? In which case, he might just leave her here to rot.

She had married in the thralls of her first real love affair and had found out very quickly that her husband was nothing more than a user, after her family connections and money. He'd never intended in any way to be monogamous. The shattering of her dreams had sent her spiraling into depression, her anger not far behind. Six months into that marriage, she had discovered one of his affairs. They had fought over it, only to have him confess to multiple affairs; then he had brutally taken his fist to her jaw. She vowed that no man would ever hit her again.

She had managed to escape from him once and had yet to come face-to-face with him again. She wouldn't be surprised if he was behind this. They had signed prenups at her father's suggestion which she then insisted on. With her divorce, that meant her ex-husband got nothing. He had fought hard on that issue, but, with only six months of marriage and the physical proof of her injuries, the divorce had been swift and easy on her side.

The judge had ruled in her favor, and her ex got nothing. Which was, as he had put it, a waste of an eighteen-month investment, and he should have at least gotten the house. But her house was worth almost one million dollars, so how he figured a year of dating and half a year of marriage should have garnered him that, she didn't know. Or her father's side, he'd been worried and upset but had been pretty caustic in his tone when saying, "I told you that he was nothing but a user."

Being told *I told you so* at that time of her life was not exactly a highlight either. Regardless, that had been almost five years ago. Surely her ex would have gotten over it by now. She hadn't seen him since, but her name and her work had recently been in the news. Had that set him off again? She was still in the same house, and she'd worried about that at the time of the divorce, but her father had set up a high-end security system.

But the trouble with her home security system was that it only worked if she were inside her home. The minute she went outside, she was fair game, and that's where she had been taken. She groaned as she shuffled on the lumpy excuse of a mattress. She closed her eyes, feeling sleepy. After all, without her watch, she was listening to her internal clock, which told her that she had woken up in the middle of the night several times, needing a bathroom.

A chamber pot was in the far corner of her cell, and she had been forced to use it several times. Even now, once again, her bladder was bursting. And yet, she'd had very little water. They had thrown a bottle in with her originally, but she'd had no food, and she didn't have a ton of body fat to begin with.

She had to escape before she was too weak to fight. If they didn't give her any food soon, that point would be facing her within hours. She got up, forced herself to the pot, where she relieved herself yet again, and then laid down on the cot once more.

Surely this nightmare would be over soon.

# CHAPTER 3

AMANDA SLEPT FOR a while, woke to use the chamber pot yet again, fell asleep only to wake up chilled on the uncomfortable cot, contemplating what day it was. She counted this as Day Two of her captivity, but she had no way to confirm that. Something odd sounded outside her door. She bolted to her feet, swaying a bit with the effort, and tiptoed to stand behind the door, her ear flat against it. She heard sobbing. Horror swept through her. She wasn't alone? It's one thing if she was the only prisoner, but to think that there might be others? It was definitely a female crying too.

A hard rap came on her door, and then a voice called out, "Step away from the door."

She frowned but immediately obeyed and stood about four feet back from where the door would open. When it did, a man dressed all in black, his rifle over his shoulder, held a tray in his hand, while a second gunman stood guard. The first thrust the tray forward, and she grabbed it immediately. Without another word, the door slammed in her face. She stared in shock at her first contact with anyone since she'd been here. Not a word, not an explanation, nothing.

Just silence. Even her neighbor no longer cried.

Horrible thoughts assaulted her mind. She shook her head, not able to handle all this … evilness.

She slowly walked back to her cot and sat down with the tray. There was a sandwich and a bowl of what appeared to be a thin soup. The food was lukewarm, but it was food. She ate slowly, knowing that she would need all the sustenance she could get, and, if she was only getting fed once a day or every other day, this wasn't enough. Still, she would survive.

They gave her another bottle of water and something in a cup too. She looked at it and frowned, wondering if it was safe to drink. Then again, was any of this food safe to eat or drink? Not that she had much choice. She picked up the sandwich, studied it carefully—old stale bread with mayo and what looked like tuna and lettuce. She took a tentative bite and then couldn't help herself from taking several bigger bites. Her hunger clawed at her, digging deep into her stomach.

She could only hope that somebody had seen her as she was snatched off the street or that someone had at least put out a call of alarm when she hadn't shown up for work the next day. Somebody should have contacted her father. And, if that had happened, he would have contacted somebody. He was high up in the government in Norway, but her birth in the States gave her dual citizenship in America. Her mother was a politician in Maine, but her parents had divorced long ago. Amanda had remained much closer to her father than her mother. Surely, between her parents, somebody would have put out a call for help.

After her initial bites, she slowed down and ate the rest of the food slowly, nibbling away at it, trying to make it last. When she'd eaten half the sandwich, she lifted a spoon and tried the soup. Canned tomato but, again, it was food. And she couldn't afford to be picky. She sipped it as slowly as she could. She needed the liquids too. She put the tray down with half the sandwich still on it but with all the soup gone. Then she picked up the cup of what? Coffee? And sniffed it. For whatever reason, she was more afraid of drugs being in the coffee than in the soup. The soup was pretty acidic, being tomato. And she hadn't tasted anything off in it. She took a tentative sip of the coffee, lukewarm but soothing.

Something else sat in the last dish on the tray and jiggled at her every move. Jell-O? That didn't make any sense, unless she was in an institution, like a hospital, where they give you the whole meal all at once. Was that a possibility? She studied her concrete cell, built of cinder blocks but missing windows. The floor was concrete as well. If she was in an institution, maybe it was a prison, and she was in solitary confinement because that's what it looked like. Or a storage room?

Then another thought came to her, and she was afraid that, if they came and took away the tray, they'd take away any remaining food too. She couldn't take that chance, so she ate the second half of her sandwich and then her dessert, polishing off the last of her coffee at the same time. She automatically checked her wrist. Old habit. But they had taken her watch, so she couldn't confirm the time or the date. But approximately an hour later she heard voices yet again. She stood with the tray in her hand as the door opened. The guard looked at it and gave a clipped nod. He took it and disappeared.

Amanda called out, "I need another chamber pot." It made him hesitate, but he still slammed the door shut. She groaned. "Surely, if this were a prison, there'd be a toilet."

As she sat on the cot again, nobody returned to talk to her. She pulled the thin blanket over her shoulders, her stomach finally full for the first time in recent memory. But now she was worried. Her mind tried hard to work on solutions to getting out of here, but, unless she was capable of fighting two armed gunmen, both apparently trained and healthy, she didn't have a hope.

Mentally she reached out and said, *If anybody out there is looking for me, please don't take too long …*

KERRICK HAD SLEPT on the plane enough that, as soon as it landed, at roughly 8:00 a.m. Monday, London time, he was energized, despite the eight-hour time difference between here and San Diego. And, with a transatlantic flight, he had also had time to review the materials given to him so that he could move forward with this op. With his carry-on bags in hand, his mind buzzed with all the intel, yet with no leads, as he tried to figure out where Dr. Berg was being held. In his head, he called out to her and said, *Amanda, I'm coming. Hold tight.*

The trouble was, he didn't really know what resources he had available to find her. The wad of cash in that envelope had been in the local currency. That helped. Also the microdot had revealed a series of bank accounts and related statements—hers, her father's, her mother's, even the corporation Amanda worked for, but Kerrick's quick review of the screenshots revealed only one year's worth of statements from each source. Yet nothing stuck out as a questionable transaction.

Kerrick had hoped his new employer would have provided him with more. Having been thrown into the deep end with little explanation or underlying supporting information, Kerrick was walking in the dark.

Still, he'd spent years walking in the shadows. He was plenty used to it.

Outside, he stopped and looked around, but nobody waited for him. He headed over to a rental car office. His envelope had also contained fake IDs. Using one of them, he quickly rented a car and headed to London. For all he knew, Amanda could have been flown to a different country by now. But this kidnapping had only recently been reported, not even fourteen hours ago, although her kidnapping had originated earlier, around 2:00 p.m. on Sunday, Paris time. Why had she been under such close scrutiny in France by Kerrick's new employer, who even now remained nameless? Why did the kidnappers take her to England at all? Scotland and Ireland were options as well as all of Europe.

Once he booked into a small cheesy motel, keeping his budget money in mind, he tossed everything onto the breakfast table to figure out his next step.

He pulled out his personal laptop, hooked up to the internet, and downloaded the research he'd gathered while in the air. He had done a background check on her history and had collected any connections Berg might have to England that he could get, courtesy of science conventions, medical conferences. Technically he didn't find much. But Amanda was a reclusive researcher, not a party girl tweeting incessantly or taking selfies and updating her dating status on Facebook.

So, while he was online, he checked his email. Almost immediately a small window opened on his laptop with a message at the bottom and a link. His first thought was that he had been hacked. Then he shook his head. Yeah, he had been hacked all right—by his new employer. He studied the message and the link. Then he clicked it.

The message gave him an account login, while the link took him to a strange site that he'd never seen before. Hesitantly but willingly, he typed in the required login information. He was logged into a server instantly. Immediately a chat window popped up.

**Welcome to England.**

**Well, I'm here, but I'm not exactly sure what I'm supposed to do.**

**If you don't know by now, then you're the wrong man for the job.** And, with that, the chat window disappeared.

He glared at it. "Well, that's fine," he said to the empty room. "It's not that I don't know what I'm doing. *Study the victim first. Then study the crime scene to get a feel for your enemy.* I'm just not exactly sure how I'm doing it yet, with my newfound parameters."

Irritated, he ignored the chat box and resumed his research, checking for any connections and further history on Amanda Berg. The web had scant information on her marriage and divorce, but, just when he had settled into studying her childhood and early school years, the chat window popped up again. He wanted to ignore it but knew that was foolish too. Words formed on the chat window.

**Time is running out.**

**Do we know what the end game is?** He typed his question, hoping his terse and direct communication with Grumpy—as he deemed his helper—if this *was* still Grumpy, would get Kerrick what he really needed: intel, not lip.

**No.**

**Father, ex-husband, company?**

**Possibly all of the above or none.**

**Studying her history online right now.**

At that, a couple more links appeared. He clicked one to see a full dossier on Amanda, much more complete than what had been given to him before on the microdot with its single sheet of data regarding Dr. Berg, some three hundred words tops. More than what he could dig up on the internet. He now read her detailed history. It was all about her schooling, her university, the awards she'd won, and the company she worked for.

The fact that she was doing cancer research could mean her kidnapper wanted Dr. Berg to treat them as a private patient, who had then kidnapped the good doctor because it was the only way they thought they could get her attention. Or possibly her kidnapper was somebody who didn't want Dr. Berg to find a cancer cure, when she seemed at a breaking point of something big per the recent newspaper articles.

Kerrick studied the various links which Grumpy had provided, realizing he was in a database. A government database that somehow Kerrick had been cleared to use. He didn't have a clue as to what his clearance would be normally. But this? Pretty awesome. He read on. … Both her parents were politicians. Immediately he asked in the chat box, **Blackmail? Kidnapping note? Ransom?**

**None yet. All things are possible.**

**Do parents know she's missing?**

**Yes, father contacted us to find daughter.**

**How did he find out?**

**Unknown to us but he refused our additional security services to protect him as he had his own private security.**

**Mother?**

**She knows but doesn't have any further info to be of assistance in this matter. Father has deployed security**

**measures of his own to watch over mother, even though they are divorced.**

**More family?**

**Only child.**

**Aunts, uncles, cousins?**

**None.**

At that, Kerrick's eyebrows raised because it was very unusual not to have *any* extended family. But who knew? It was what it was. While he read more of her expanded dossier, the chat sent a couple more links, which Kerrick immediately pulled up and read. **I need information**, he typed.

**About what?**

**Her coworkers. Is she close to anybody in particular at work? The state of her actual research. Is she truly close to making a breakthrough, or is that just media hype in the newspapers? Is she working for any special funding group?**

**Back in five.** And then whoever was on the other end of their chat left.

Frowning, Kerrick quickly returned to reading everything else he had been given on Amanda and realized that she'd been seen in a blue four-door vehicle, not the lorry that had taken her away initially, yet both had been on the ferry. Or at least he thought the original lorry used in the kidnapping had been with the blue car on the ferry. Somebody had tried to track her using the car's license plate, but the vehicle was lost on the other side of the ferry crossing at Dover.

He reviewed the other photos in the brown envelope but saw none from the ferry crossing. Supposedly, she'd been laid down in the back seat and covered up, as if asleep, to give her an almost normal appearance, so as not to alert the ferry authorities. And that made Kerrick wonder just how correct their intel was.

In the chat box, he quickly asked that question and then sent a second question about tracking the vehicle itself. When the responses came back, an image was attached, showing a birthmark high on her cheek, near her right eye. It correlated to the same facial mark found in his file.

**Both vehicles lost almost immediately in Dover, the lorry and the blue car. License plates no longer visible, so we assumed they were switched. Either switched vehicles or switched license plates.**

Kerrick nodded. All too often, that was an easy option.

**Not close to any coworkers. Works solo on her own research. Reliable sources state she is on the verge of finding a cancer cure. While she has been awarded several grants over the years, her current funding group is her employer, Scion Labs.**

Well, that was not much.

As he learned more about the kidnapping victim, who this woman was, he found nothing in the files or in his research to dislike. She was known as a champion of lost causes—being a member of both the dance club and the genius club in her school years as a teenager—which led to her being very popular, as she helped everybody to meet and to organize various social parties, trying to get the wallflowers off the wall and onto the dance floor.

He smiled at that. Of course she'd been a social butterfly type coming from her political family of origin, but obviously, as an adult, she could be an introvert too and have hidden depths if she was also a chemist, working on cancer research. And that sent him down another rabbit hole. He went to the chat box again. **What prompted cancer research?**

**Best friend died in college.**

**Name?**

**Alice Durnham.**
**Should have been in the dossier.**
**Ask and you shall receive.**

He snorted, wondering if this was still Grumpy but reformed, or if Kerrick was getting bounced between five different people, like some call center located wherever on this planet. Regardless he resumed his own research into Alice Durnham. And, indeed, she had struggled with breast cancer as a young woman, not knowing she had the disease until it was too late to treat.

It had affected Amanda deeply. She had lost a lot of her bubbliness since then, and she had changed the direction of her research to find a cure for cancer. Something interesting in that same vein had been how she had also lost another friend. It was briefly touched upon, but this other mutual friend had introduced her to her future husband. Kerrick searched for the name of the friend and couldn't find it. He typed in the chat box once more, and the reply came one minute later.

**Bridgette Hampton. Died in a car accident. Ruled an accident. No reason to consider otherwise.**
**How soon after introducing the husband?**
**One month.**
**Would help the bonding.**
**Yes.**
**Any connection from ex-husband to any extremist groups?**
**Under investigation but nothing points in that direction at this time.**

Aah, so the chat box people didn't have all the answers. He frowned because he really didn't want to find limits to what he needed to know. He quickly typed in another question. **Any connection to anything suspicious?**

Lots.

**Such as?**

He received a list of associations that the ex-husband had dabbled in. Everything from vegan groups to gun groups to divorce groups. He frowned as he thought about that. **That's a lot of nothing.**

Yes.

Cover?

Possibly.

**Location of ex-husband and whereabouts for the last thirty to seventy-two hours?**

**Was at work Friday. Went missing over the weekend. Has a new lady friend. Possibly they went on a trip.**

**It's Monday.**

**Hasn't shown up for work.**

**Suspicious.**

Yes.

**Father?**

**Looking into potential blackmailers.**

**Should have had a ransom note by now.**

**Not necessarily.**

**Let me know if you find the ex or if the father gets a blackmail demand.**

**Okay.**

And it went on and on as Kerrick kept delving in, trying to get more and more information. **We need a location in England. She was being followed by someone, who reported it to her father, I presume. Do we have that info? Can we contact the security detail?**

**No. Not available. We have nothing else.**

He sighed and groaned. **She could be anywhere.**

**Yes.**

**That's not helpful.**

**No.**

**Tracking device on her?**

**No.**

**Tracking device on the blue four-door?**

**No.**

**Health issues that might necessitate her needing medication?**

**No.**

He groaned. **Satellite?**

**Absolutely.**

**I want to see the image from the day she was taken, and I also want the camera feeds from the bridge as she came off the ferry. I want to follow those two vehicles.**

**Just a moment.**

**Also need weapons and tactical gear.**

When the response came he stared. **Already loaded in car.**

Really? He didn't want to check now. He'd have to continue to trust. He continued to go through the paperwork that he'd been given and realized that he should have picked up food before he came here. He got up, walked over to the window, and stared around at his nearby surroundings. A small diner was at the end of the block. That would do. **Grabbing food**, he typed in the chat box. **Back in ten.**

Then he quickly locked up the motel room and headed across the street and into the small diner. There, he ordered a meal to-go, coffee, and picked up several muffins and some doughnuts. Sugar was always good for a hit of energy as long as in moderation. Back in his room, he still had no answer from the chat window. He sat down with the laptop in front of him and ate. Then he cleaned up his garbage and sat back, doing more research.

Time was wasting, but, if they didn't have any intel, even England was way too damn big for Kerrick to start knocking on doors. When his laptop beeped, he clicked his computer to see the satellite feed. Then he clicked on the chat window. **I need remote access to an imaging program.**

There was silence for a long moment while he continued to study the feed, and then he was given a set of logins and a link. He quickly hit the link and logged in. Opening up that video, he zoomed the images to a much higher pixel count to see exactly what he needed to look at. Sure enough, the woman "asleep" on the back seat of the car under surveillance had a scar on her right cheek. The mark was on one of the earlier photos of Amanda that he had, but he had missed it on the first go-around because he had only looked at the background in her picture, taking in the scenery behind her head. But on further examination, there was a definite triangular or kind of heart-shaped scar on her right cheekbone, high and close to her ear. It happened to be that side of her facing up in the photo too. She appeared to be drugged. He did a quick perusal, studying the vehicle, writing down the type and the make and that a rear light was broken.

**Check for an accident report**, he typed into the chat box. Then he kept on searching the satellite feed, going through every angle on that ferry, trying to get something on the driver. But all Kerrick got was dark hair on a hairy arm by the open window. He was the only other person in the vehicle.

**No accident on file regarding ferry passengers for that date and time using data available and as reported.**

**Single driver with "sleeping" passenger confirmed by birthmark as Amanda Berg**, he typed into the chat box.

But then he stopped and wondered about the lorry

parked right behind the car on the ferry. He zoomed out, taking a look at the distance between them. A transport truck would make a lot more sense for a kidnapping, where she wouldn't be visible. So, was this the lorry that had first taken her? Then, before reaching the ferry, they had moved her to the blue car, like she was sleeping, instead of remaining in the back of a lorry, where an unconscious woman would look particularly suspicious, should the ferry authorities demand a search?

And then the kidnappers transferred her back into a lorry—or *the* lorry—after the ferry landed? Or was this lorry just a decoy? Either way, these kidnappers had done this before. Kerrick pressed Play on the video feed, moving it forward, and the car went ahead, exiting the ferry, with the lorry following. They both took the first exit, and then another vehicle jumped in between the car and the lorry, making Kerrick even more suspicious. Or it could be a total random event.

As he kept watching, the video feed cut off.

He immediately asked via the chat box for access to the transit cameras at that intersection. Their chat continued with more links followed by more links. He kept looking, following the car, but, for at least one mile, blank spaces and blind spots filled the camera feed. The transit cameras could only do so much.

He kept following the video until he found yet another blind spot, and, when he came up on the other side of that suspicious part of the feed, the car was gone. So was the lorry and the middle car. He backtracked and looked at the online map he had pulled up into a new tab to see where else the car could have headed. He kept on searching down the optional roads on various feeds and then asked for another feed. He quickly clicked on the new feed and reviewed it.

He needed to grab all these logins to put into a master file to memorize for other cases. He didn't want to keep asking for access. Almost at this train of thought, the chat window's new message read **Watch your back** and then disappeared.

Chat was gone. To the empty room he whispered, "Thanks for that." Luckily he had some feeds still open on his laptop.

He studied the blind spot and noted another road heading off to the side. He picked up the next transit camera intersection four blocks away, but he saw no sign of the blue car anywhere in the next hour's worth of feed. That bothered him, but he couldn't get a view of that corner. It was about forty minutes away from where he sat. He quickly packed up his laptop and the rest of the equipment that he had, as well as his ready bag, just in case, and then headed out to his rental vehicle.

He drove to the point where the blue car had been lost in the traffic feeds. He still had the camera feeds up on his laptop, so he could double-check the area around him. He drove forward and around several blocks. Then, with his instincts prodding him, he pulled off onto the shoulder and got out. It was now three o'clock in the afternoon, Monday. *Damn it! Where had the time gone?*

He noted traffic was everywhere, and it was a hell of an intersection to try to disappear into. But, at the time of the supposed kidnapper's Dover crossing, it would have been about 7:00 that Sunday evening. So, if this were truly the kidnapper's car driving outside of London, about 9:00 p.m. that Sunday, as evidenced by the time stamp on the satellite feeds and on the street cameras, then that vehicle pulled safely off the shoulder here. Kerrick walked up and down the first hundred yards from where the camera went blind, checking on both sides of the road. He stood for a moment with his hands on his head, swearing.

What had happened to the car? It hadn't gone forward, and it hadn't been seen on the other side. But then he remembered the lorry. How big was that damn lorry?

He got into his rental and searched his feeds and confirmed his initial assessment—it was a large lorry, like a moving truck. And then he knew what had happened. He quickly zoomed in on the feeds, picked the ID number off the lorry and its license plate number, and ran a search. Because, of all the things, if the blue car wasn't here, and he couldn't find any sign of it, that meant it wasn't here. There was no ravine to have gone down; there was no cliff to have gone over; there were no houses with garages. Nothing but straight traffic thoroughfares.

There were subdivisions all around, but no exits here accessed them. Which meant the lorry had pulled ahead, and the car had driven up on a ramp into the back and could even now be inside that damn lorry. He needed help. He picked up his disposable phone and quickly dialed its only saved number. When the other voice asked for his identification, he gave it and said, "I need the chat."

Instantly the chat window opened up, and he gave them the license plate and the lorry ID number. **Find that sucker.** Then he typed alongside that **The car's inside it.**

The chat box disappeared for a long moment while he drove around and parked on higher ground, where he could get a better view of the overlaying area. The lorry could have driven for another eighteen hours across country, but he suspected—now that the car had been hidden inside the lorry—that the kidnappers were close to their true destination.

So they had driven to another place near London, where they were probably safe to park and able to work there. But where did one park a huge lorry like that? It had a company's logo on one side, but, as he saw from the various video camera feeds, it had a different logo on the other side. So it had been repurposed from its original intent, which made a lot of sense but would also throw people off.

Different witnesses would give differing reports to the authorities, sullying their veracity. *Smart move, from the criminal's mind-set.* He hadn't seen anybody try that before, but it made sense. It also gave credence to his working theory that the lorry had swallowed up the car. Using the live camera feeds, he backed up the feeds and then quickly searched through them for the appropriate time stamp; he needed to see where that sucker went.

*There.* And it did drive down near here. It headed through that intersection, then picked up again on the main route, and headed forward. It was slow and painstaking to get through these rudimentary street-camera feeds. The software used for a video game for home use had more viability than these city street cameras. Kerrick shook his head at that.

Just then the chat window offered a new link. He quickly tapped on it to see the lorry turning off into a large parking lot, and its corresponding street address popped up below. A trucking company. Another good idea. Hide one lorry among many other lookalikes. He immediately entered the company's address into his GPS and drove. He didn't know where the hell that vehicle was now, but he needed to find it. The kidnappers might not have unloaded the car yet, but they sure as hell would have unloaded the passenger— unless she was already dead.

# CHAPTER 4

AMANDA WOKE UP bitterly cold, her body shivering, trying to warm up in her cool cell by rubbing her hands along her arms. She followed the innate wisdom of her internal clock and deemed this the next morning. But how could she tell for sure? It could be just the continuation of what she had earlier deemed as her second day here. Or … hell. Still her first day here. Actually that made more sense. Time would drag by here, she suspected.

She shook her head. The drugs and lack of light messed with her senses.

She had to once again get up to relieve her bladder. And found that the pot had been emptied. Did they do that at night, when she slept? That gave credence to this being a new day, Day 2? Or Day 3 of captivity for her?

She frowned; somehow she'd slept through the night and hadn't even heard her visitor. That wasn't good. But her next thought was not any better. The only way for that to have happened was either the room was gassed or her food had been drugged.

Surprise, surprise.

She didn't know how much longer they were planning on keeping her here. There hadn't been another sound or another voice crying since she'd heard the first one. That was disturbing.

Then she turned bitterly cold, both inside and out. She laid here for a long moment, distracting herself by listening intently, but there was nothing to hear. She got up and systematically walked from wall to wall, trying to listen to the other side, tapping to see if she could find a hollow space in the walls—or to hear tapping in return from another captive like her. But she found no weakness in the walls and no neighbors.

Then, back at the door, she held her ear against the wood and could hear something banging outside. She tested the doorknob, but it was locked. There was no opening or window in it, so she had no way to see out. She studied the door hinges, wondering if she could take it apart. But she didn't have any tools. Nothing here could even possibly undo those screws. And they were pretty intense-looking screws. A drill would be required, and, if the screws were really old, like the rest of this place seemed to be, then they were probably rusted, and she couldn't do anything with them anyway. The pins were also long and deep and rusty looking so no budging those.

Just then a hard pounding came at the door. She jumped back in shock, and a voice called out, "Stand away from the door."

Shivering in the cold, with her arms wrapped around her, she stepped back a few feet and waited until the door opened. It was the same man who had delivered the tray of food to her once, but he carried no food, only held a gun this time, which he pointed at her, while another man in a white lab coat stepped inside.

She stared at her boss in shock. "Dr. Hinkleman?"

He gave her a fat smile and nodded. "Glad you're awake enough to know my name."

She stared at him in bewilderment. "Why am I here?"

"Because you won't do what you're told," he said in exasperation.

She shook her head. "I've been working under you for years. Of course I'm doing what I'm told. What is this all about?" She threw her arms wide open. "Do you have any idea how cold it is in here?" At that, her teeth started to chatter too.

Immediately the doctor frowned, turned, and barked an order in another language to the man behind her. Who barked an order to somebody else, somebody out of her sight and probably standing in the hallway. Of course nobody would leave her alone long enough to retrieve a blanket for her, but her mind spun off in a million directions, trying to figure out what had been said. Why was her boss here? Where was she?

"What is this about?" she asked.

"A couple things," Hinkleman said smoothly. "Your work, for one. Somebody who doesn't want you, for another, and somebody who is happy to get back at your father, for a third. I'm basically collecting on two points and getting what I want at the same time. Bonus."

She took a deep, slow breath, trying hard to calm her pounding heart as she realized just how many people could be involved in this. "Are you saying you coordinated with two groups of people to have me brought here?"

"I coordinated with a lot more than that," he said. "But it doesn't really matter because you're here. I've been paid times two and get your research for my own."

"If you wanted my research, you know it was yours anyway, based upon the employee agreement I signed when I hired on with Scion Labs. They get ownership of any patents or trademarks, etcetera, of my creation while under Scion Labs employ," she said, struggling to focus on one of these issues. "This doesn't make any sense. The one who wants to get rid of me would be my ex-husband, but he should have done that before I signed the divorce papers. The one trying to get back at my father ..." She turned to the doctor and snapped, "Could be anybody in the world."

"Keep your temper. But you certainly nailed the people, yes. As for your research, you haven't been letting me know about all of it, have you?"

She frowned blankly at him but knew he wasn't fooled. "You know that I'm not supposed to give you anything until we have surety," she said slowly. "And obviously I haven't hit that point, or I would have told you."

"It doesn't matter," he said, "because somebody else who works with you told me all about it. And I'm very disappointed you didn't tell me first. Now you'll be sorry too."

KERRICK PULLED INTO a large parking lot, past the one he was interested in. He had slowed as he had driven by the first one, but he confirmed it as his destination as he saw a lot of lorries parked outside. He pulled up, parked on the side of the building housing Hope Rims Company, and pretended to walk toward its office.

Instead, he dodged past, as if heading to the loading zone. There, he hopped over the fence into the neighboring property and snuck up against the building for the trucking company. He tried to listen in on any conversations in the parking lot, mostly drivers razzing and joking about how their weekend plans had worked out. That wasn't exactly what Kerrick cared about.

He studied the vehicles parked in the large lot, waited until the men outside loaded up and pulled out, and then walked among the lorries, looking for one in particular. It was the fourth one from the back along the fence, but it was pulled forward so the back could be accessed. He took several photos, sent them to his contact, and checked that it had the expected license plate number and the right lorry ID number. Then he swung open the large rear door to the storage area and hopped inside.

It was completely empty. Of course it was. Knowing the car was long gone, he checked to see if there was any sign that it had been here. He found a few drops of oil. He stopped, took a picture of it, took a sample of it using a Q-tip in a Ziploc bag, and popped it into his pocket, just in case it might be of need later. Then found more oil at the opposite end of the lorry. *Strange.* He took samples of it too.

He slipped out, shut the door softly, and walked up to the front of the cab. It was unlocked, so he hopped inside now, quite content that nobody could see him unless they came to move this particular lorry. He checked the logs in the glove box. The insurance was in the name of the company on whose property he sat, which made sense.

Kerrick thought about the traffic feeds and realized he hadn't checked the side panels of the lorry. It's quite possible somebody had changed the logo. He took several photographs of the insurance papers and the logbooks, but nothing here noted that this lorry had taken the ferry over from the mainland. *Interesting.*

Yet an employee of this company was more likely involved in the kidnapping itself, not so much the company. The employee just needed his employer's lorry. Kerrick made his way back outside and checked the logos on each side of the lorry. And, sure enough, one side had the permanent company logo painted thereon. On the other side? The same logo replication. Whatever had been there before was no longer present. It must have been a large plastic or magnetic sign that the employee could easily put on and take down again. *Again, interesting.*

Kerrick quickly walked around the parking lot, took several license plates photos from other vehicles, and then stepped up toward the main office. A young woman sat behind the counter, typing. He waited until she was free, then smiled, and told her that he was looking for the driver of lorry 714.

She looked up at him in surprise. "Why?" she asked suspiciously.

He gave her a winning smile and said, "He's a friend of mine." It was almost comical how much relief crossed her face when she heard that.

"That's Jimmy's lorry," she said. "He knows everybody." She waved her hand. "You just missed him."

"Surely that wasn't him who just drove out?" he asked with an exaggerated frown.

She nodded. "He's got a delivery down the road. He should be back in a couple hours."

He looked outside, checked his watch, and looked outside again. "How late are you open?"

"If you can't wait, just come back," she said. "The office closes at six. But Jimmy will return the lorry whenever he's done, if it's later than that."

"Or I could check him out at the job. I was hoping to make plans for the coming weekend."

"He's gone to the commercial growers up the road with

a big load of fertilizer and chemicals to drop off."

Kerrick waved his thanks, stepped out of the office, heading for his rental. He drove up the road, looking for the growers, found the location, and plugged it into his GPS. He pulled off to the side in time to witness the men unloading the delivery.

He didn't know which one was Jimmy or who the other guy was. From his vehicle, he took several photos of their faces and quickly sent them off to his one and only contact on his burner phone, with a note saying he was looking for Jimmy, the regular driver of lorry 714 which had come across the ferry. Just an update for Beta.

Kerrick figured that *his people* would get to him as soon as they had anything further or something new. At least he hoped so. He wasn't used to having zero contact with anyone in person and just waiting until things were deep-sixed in the internet, the equivalent of filing things in the circular file. On the other hand, there was a certain amount of freedom without having to check in.

He waited in his vehicle until the delivery men were more or less done. Then one of the men walked into the storefront. Kerrick walked in after him and listened as he talked to the women up front. They called the dark-haired man Tom, which meant Jimmy was the one outside and still at the lorry. Kerrick walked toward Jimmy, standing beside the lorry, lighting up a cigarette.

Kerrick gave Jimmy a smile, pointing at his lorry, and said, "Hey, didn't I just see you on the ferry coming from the mainland yesterday?"

Jimmy ground out the cigarette and gave him a blank stare. "Not me. Not my rig."

Kerrick backed up, looked at the number on the rig, and

said, "Same tag, same type lorry, wrong number though. It was seven-one-four that I saw on the ferry."

Jimmy shook his graying head. "Well, that's my rig, but I wasn't driving it over there, that's for sure. And not on no Sunday."

"Well, it was definitely on the ferry. Pretty sure you were the driver." Kerrick frowned as if he was really confused, reaching up to scratch his temple. "But maybe not. It was definitely your lorry though." Then he walked to the other side and said, "Part of the reason I noticed was it had two different logos. One on each side of the lorry."

Jimmy gave him another blank look.

"You don't know anything about it?" Kerrick asked in surprise.

Jimmy shook his head. "No, not me. You must be talking about somebody else."

"Maybe not you. But it was your lorry. Maybe I'll head back to the trucking office and see who that was then."

"Why do you care?" Jimmy asked.

"Oh, I care," Kerrick said. "Had a little bit of a confab with that vehicle."

"What kind of confab?" Jimmy asked, getting upset. "My lorry's not banged up at all."

"Didn't say it was a lorry confab, did I?" Kerrick said.

"Well, if you had a dust-up with a driver, you'd have known it wasn't me."

"Good point," he said. "I think I'll go find that lorry. Your company's yard is just a couple miles from here, isn't it?" Then he pulled up his phone, nodded, and said, "Yep, I'll find out who that driver was."

"When was that again?"

Jimmy didn't appear to understand what was going on,

which kind of put him into the *might be innocent* category. But, at the same time, Kerrick had seen a lot of men who could lie so well that you'd never know. He gave Jimmy the time and date of the ferry crossing per the pictures he had on his phone.

Jimmy shook his head over and over again. "I was home with my wife. My rig was in the yard."

Just to prove the point, Kerrick brought up the picture of the lorry and the ferry number on his phone, then held it up to Jimmy.

Jimmy was flabbergasted. He just stared, his jaw dropping. "Well," he roared, "that son of a bitch."

"You want to clarify?"

"Hell no, I don't," Jimmy said. "That suffices to say that somebody I know took that lorry when he shouldn't have."

"Well, that might be," Kerrick said, "but it's your assigned lorry. Do you want to get in trouble or should your buddy?"

Jimmy glared at him. "Why? Who are you, and why do you care?"

With a hard smile, Kerrick pulled out one of his many IDs and held it up. "Somebody who cares," he said. His voice went low and hard. "Whoever you lent that lorry to was up to no good. Illegal activities with that lorry have been photographed."

Jimmy's face blanched. "I didn't have nothing to do with that," he snapped.

"Bullshit," Kerrick said. "If that's not you driving that lorry, you obviously know who is." He pulled his phone down and checked through his photos and then, finding one of the cars ahead, he held it up and said, "And do you recognize that car?"

Jimmy sucked in a breath. It seemed he knew a hell of a lot more than he had said so far. Slowly he nodded his head. "I do," he said, "but I don't know what the hell's going on."

"And why is that?"

"Because the guy who owns that car doesn't work for the company anymore."

"But let me guess, he's friends with the driver who borrowed your lorry?"

Jimmy winced.

"And they paid you to look the other way. Is that it?"

"Yeah," he said, shamefaced. "But I thought it was just to pick up a few extra moving jobs on the weekend or after hours during the week."

"*Moving*, indeed," Kerrick said starkly. "I wonder if you have any idea what they were moving this time."

Jimmy shook his head. "No, I don't think I want to."

"No, you don't," Kerrick said. "But I'll tell you anyway. We've got a missing woman, and she'd been ID'd in the back of this car in front of your lorry, which then picked up the car and hauled it in the back of the lorry, moving this kidnapped woman somewhere else."

Jimmy stepped back, his face turning beet red, his hand at his chest. For a moment, Kerrick thought Jimmy would have a heart attack, watching him carefully, but eventually Jimmy caught his breath and then in a panic said, "I didn't have nothing to do with that."

"And we're back to the same point where we were earlier," Kerrick said coolly. "Who was driving the lorry?"

Jimmy worked a hand through the wispy white hairs at the top of his head, obviously not sure what to do.

"That's fine," Kerrick said. "I can haul you in and will question you and your family as to what connections you have to this kidnapped woman."

Immediately Jimmy backed up several paces. "I didn't have nothing to do with it." He held up his hands in front of his chest, waving Kerrick back. "Nothing, you hear me?"

"I want a name," Kerrick said. He pulled up his phone and quickly took a snap of Jimmy's face. "Just so we can find you whenever we want you," he said.

At that, Jimmy started to talk. "Stanley. Stanley Warrick," he said. "The guy used to work at the trucking company."

"So he's the one who owns the blue car?"

Jimmy nodded.

"And he's the one driving the lorry onto the ferry last night?"

Again Jimmy nodded.

"But he's no longer employed by your company, right?"

"Yeah, he was fired about six months ago."

"Why?"

Jimmy took several deep long breaths and finally blurted out the truth. "He was taking the rigs, disabling the GPS, and driving them after-hours."

"Interesting," Kerrick said. "And, since he got fired, your friend is now getting you to cover for him while he does the same thing. Right?"

"Yeah, but honestly, I didn't think it was anything like this."

"Did your employer ever find out what this Stanley guy was doing with the rigs?"

Jimmy shook his head. "Not back then. But it was nothing like this. Stanley didn't go very far. We figured he was just bringing over and distributing shipments of imported illegal goods."

"Such as?"

"Maybe some wines that didn't have the proper papers, maybe some easily sold items …" Jimmy looked at Kerrick, still half panicked, and said, "I didn't have anything to do with that shit. … I promise."

"Promises don't mean anything when a woman's life is in danger," Kerrick said. "Who else would be involved from the trucking company?"

At that, Jimmy stopped, looked at Kerrick, looked again at the storefront where his coworker still was, and said, "I don't think there's anybody else."

The way Jimmy was eyeing the storefront meant this had to be about Tom too. "Well, there's at least two vehicles directly involved," Kerrick said. "Stanley's car had to be driven by somebody because you just said Stanley was driving the stolen lorry. So, if two people are driving around, chances are more people are involved."

Jimmy shook his head, his wispy hair flying around as he said, "I don't think so."

"Well, somebody's got to be looking the other way. What about the extra mileage on the rigs?"

Jimmy's face turned bloodred, and he looked to see if his partner had come out of the store yet. He then faced Kerrick. "Sometimes I change the mileage back a bit."

"Really? And nobody's thought to check them? And nobody's thought to check with your rigs during the weekend or at night?"

Jimmy flushed and looked downward.

Kerrick nodded and said, "You disabled the LoJack, didn't you?"

"Only a couple times early on. When I was afraid they'd check. But they never did so …"

"And they don't track the GPS on the lorries and check it against mileage records?"

"Not yet," he said glumly. "But they probably will now that you're here."

"And how long have you been doing this?" Kerrick snapped. "Do you always steal from your employer?"

"I've been here forty years," Jimmy snapped back. "I got another year, and then I'm out. Do you think they'll give me anything but a handshake and a pat on the back that says thanks?"

"And why do you deserve more?" Kerrick asked. "Did they not give you a paycheck all these years? And I presume a decent one because you stayed."

Jimmy blinked several times at that. And he shrugged. "But I don't have enough to live on if I can't work."

"So were you involved in Stanley's smuggling operations too?"

Behind him came a voice, saying, "What are you talking about? Smuggling?"

The voice was young and light. Tom was half whistling as he walked toward them. "Anybody who knows Jimmy would know that in no way would he do anything wrong." Then the young guy grinned at Kerrick, held out his hand— a hairy hand full of black hair—and said, "Now, me, Tom Paine, well, you know what? I might have been known to nick a few things in my time."

*And Tom must have driven Stanley's blue car onto the ferry with Amanda unconscious in the back seat. So that third vehicle could very well have been driven by my man Jimmy here.*

Jimmy opened the cab door and said, "Come on, Tom. We got to go."

"Now we're not in that big a hurry," Tom said. "What's

the rush?"

Jimmy shot a dark look toward Kerrick. "Nothing. We're late, and I want to go home." He hopped in, slammed the door, and turned on the engine.

Tom lifted a hand and said, "Hey, my ride's leaving. Anytime you want to talk to me, give me a shout."

"At what number?" Kerrick asked drily. But, to his surprise, the kid peeled off a number. Kerrick quickly added it to his cell phone and nodded. "Maybe I'll do that. How long have you worked for them?"

"About six months," he said with a big grin. "It's a really good paycheck. I like the hours, and I like the work. They're really very good to deal with."

"So, you wouldn't be involved in anything shady then, would you?" Kerrick's voice was low and curious.

Tom opened up the passenger side, just as Jimmy attempted to move forward. Tom hopped up before it took off on him, and he said, "Nah, no way. The owners, they're really good to deal with."

"Yeah, you must be related to them."

Tom chuckled. "I am. They're my grandparents."

No wonder Jimmy didn't want to speak up. He was nearing retirement age, didn't want to screw that up. But he was already in enough hot water letting Stanley, who was fired, still use the company's lorry, while Jimmy covered for Stanley by tweaking the mileage records. Now Jimmy surely didn't want to name the bosses' own grandkid as their accomplice to a kidnapping, not to mention bringing up the smuggling issue as well.

And, with that, the two lying employees tore off down the road.

# CHAPTER 5

AMANDA WOKE UP again, trusting her internal clock to remain accurate, shivering once again. The windowless cold gray walls stared back at her. Her stomach churned violently. Nothing was more unsettling than knowing you were getting sick unless it was knowing that you were locked up as a prisoner in a dark cold room with only a full pee pot to throw up in. Just the thought of getting up to hang her head over the top of that thing made her balk. The smell alone would make her erupt violently.

Trying to focus on anything else, she laid in bed, gasping, willing her gut to calm down. Finally she was forced to sit up, hanging her legs over the edge, dropping her head between her knees, hoping to still the stream. Was it the little bit of drugged food they'd given her, or was it just the lack of food? She had tried so hard not to eat, but it was impossible when the hunger got to her. And, of course, these assholes knew that. Hinkleman also hadn't returned. He had just laughed at her circumstances and had walked out even when she had cried after him, "What do you want?"

He had lifted a hand goodbye and left.

The fact that he was getting paid several times over to keep her captive was mind-blowing. She hadn't made a name for herself. Not yet. Her father had, as a politician. As had her mother. And sure, Amanda wanted to feel the rewards for her research work on cancer. Several of her patients had gone into remission after taking her drug, but, of course, her patients were of the four-legged variety, not the humans who she needed to try her cure on.

But getting human trials approved was something else. And she didn't understand why Hinkleman would be upset that she was to the point of applying for those. Couldn't he appreciate what she had done? His name went on all the papers anyway. Although hers would go on the papers too. She was his underling.

Was that it? Was he not willing to share the glory? Pretty upsetting if that's the case because he already had several awards in his name, but they were from decades ago. Yet he clung to them and reminded everybody of them almost weekly. But this level of curing-cancer research, of course, was where everybody wanted to be. A cure for cancer was the Holy Grail. Why wouldn't Dr. Hinkleman appreciate that, no matter who found the cure?

Even before all her formal upper-level schooling, she'd been very young when joining the Mensa group. There she'd met many people who were doing awesome things in life, inspiring her to do even more. After Alice's death, Amanda had chosen to work on improving the human condition by finding a cure for breast cancer.

As she sat in the darkness, she could feel the tears well up, and she called out to her dead friend. "Alice, I sure hope you're doing well in a better place. There's a good chance I could be joining you soon."

Of course Amanda heard no answer. There was never any answer. She'd been talking to Alice since her death. She knew, every once in a while, her coworkers caught her mumbling to herself. And that was fine. The problem was, she was mumbling to a specific person, knowing full well that she wouldn't get an answer back but needing to converse with her anyway. After all, Alice was why Amanda did this. To save others like Alice. She'd been so young when she had been diagnosed with breast cancer, of all things.

In Amanda's mind, she'd always thought that breast cancer belonged to middle-aged or older women who'd already had their two-point-five kids and the breasts themselves had been worn out and used up. But instead, her friend was only twenty-six and yet to be pregnant, and she had died so soon afterward. How was that fair? And, of course, it wasn't, but Amanda's situation wasn't fair either. Life was a bitch sometimes.

Just then she heard a gentle tap, but she didn't understand from where. She hopped out of bed, instantly woozy and unsure on her feet, stopping to steady herself, and still not knowing what time it was exactly in the darkness. She was losing track of most of her senses now.

She walked over to one wall and tapped gently. Nothing. She walked to the next, tapped again and again, and at the door she tapped as well. And just as she went to do that on the next wall, another tap sounded, but it came from the ceiling above her. She slowly stepped onto her cot, steadying herself again, not surprised by her weakness, and tapped back. There was almost a startled sensation, and then two more taps came. She tapped twice back.

At least this way, they knew that she had heard and that they were communicating. Didn't mean that they knew *what* they were communicating, but she'd take any sign of human existence that she could.

When the taps came back three times, she got a little pissed, but she tapped three times back as well. Her worst nightmare was of a child playing up there, letting people know that the floor was talking to them. And then she noted the ensuing series of taps and breaks. And it repeated over and over again. She caught her breath, dragged her mind back to the Morse code that she had learned when interested in navy life. She realized that somebody was signaling to her. She listened to it tapped out over and over again: H-E-L.

Her heart sank and her eyes closed when the *P* came.

She didn't know what to say. She tapped her reply slowly. *Yes, please help me.*

Another startled moment could be heard from above and then another set of taps. *Can't* came back. And then *Help me?*

Tears dripped down Amanda's cheeks as she realized that, indeed, somebody else was being held here too, another prisoner, not just the crying woman heard earlier on Amanda's same floor but also above her. She tapped back slowly. *Can't. Locked in.*

The answer came as *Me too.*

Needing to know that somebody was out there, somebody who maybe could tell her father, she tapped out her name and added *Chemist kidnapped.*

What came back was a name. *Brandon Coleman. Kidnapped.*

And then the next part broke her heart. *Ten years old.*

She screamed a cry of rage, a cry of pain and anger. A little boy was up there, a child held captive. Like her. She sent another message back. *Why?*

*Father bad.*

*Not.*

*They say so.*

*Doesn't matter. Stay strong.*

*You?*

*Ex-husband mad at me. Also some enemy of my father in-volved.* Not sure what to say next, she sank onto her cot. When she heard footsteps outside, she quickly stood and tapped *Quiet. Someone's coming.* The last thing she wanted was for anybody to know that they were communicating.

Someone pounded on her door.

When the order came for her to stand back from the doorway, she climbed off her cot, automatically took several steps backward, and stood at attention.

The door opened, and Hinkleman walked in. He glared at her. "We need you."

She opened her eyes wide. "Of course," she said. "What do you need me for?"

"Your notes," he snapped. "They don't make any sense."

She frowned. "If they don't make any sense, it's because you're not following them. Or … someone has altered them."

"You?"

She shook her head rapidly. "You know I would never corrupt the data. That's everything to me."

He stared at her for a long moment and then, without warning, smacked her hard across the face. The blow sent her reeling, and she collapsed on the cot. He turned and walked out again.

She lay here, her anger returning. Memories of her ex hitting her added to her ire. Yet through it all she knew she hadn't heard the hard *snick* on the lock as the door was slammed behind her.

Slowly, with her ear against the door, she pushed down the handle and tugged the door toward her. She only opened it a little bit to see if anybody would slam the door in her face. But nobody appeared to be outside her door, at least not in the three feet before her door. The hallway was disjointed, if it were a hallway at all. By the time she took three steps and reached the next corner, she peeked around, and she could now see that her short hallway joined a long and dank hallway, but faint running lights ran above her on the ceiling. Multiple doors were on both sides. This hallway was also completely empty.

She had waited for one opportunity, and she took it.

THE TRUCKING COMPANY had closed for the day at 6:00 p.m., and it was almost 7:00 now. Kerrick sat in his vehicle in an empty lot several blocks away and quickly researched the employee names he had been given from the very helpful front-desk lady. All it took was the mention of Stanley Warwick, and she wanted to do everything possible to make sure nobody was doing that again. Kerrick had already sent those names to his contact. When he received a text message to **Call**, he picked up his phone and waited for the tumblers to connect him to a secure line.

Then he asked, "What's up?"

"One of the trucking company employees used to work for a biochemical research company," said the quiet voice on the other end of the call.

The voice this time wasn't Beta's, his old buddy. Yet another new voice without a name in this new government division.

"He was a delivery driver for them until he got fired six months ago."

*Tom Paine.* "The owner's grandkid. And?"

"It's the same company she worked for."

Instantly he went "Yes!" This is exactly what they needed. It was a break, and it was something to blow open this case. "Perfect," he said. "I need to know everything about the biochemical research company. I want to know all the details, no matter how small."

"It won't help much. It's in Paris."

"Everything helps. She was kidnapped after work in front of that building. Every little tidbit helps," Kerrick said firmly. And then he swore. "I don't want to take the time to hop over there, but I might have to."

"Tell us what you want."

He ran off a list of all the questions he wanted answered about the company. Then, when he finally ran out of steam, he said, "And get it to me later tonight."

The voice laughed. "You don't ask for much, do you?"

"You want the girl saved, don't you?"

There was silence for an instant. "You'll get your answers," the voice said, and then it rang off.

Kerrick wished he could send a message to Amanda herself, letting her know that somebody was coming for her. Letting her know that somebody cared. Because, in spite of himself, he was starting to care about this victim. He'd been on several teams that had rescued kidnapped victims before, but there was just something about that clear and direct gaze of Amanda's ... That purpose in her eyes, that sense of self, as if to say *I know exactly what I'll do. I know how I'll do it, and, Cancer, you better damn watch out because I'm coming for you.*

He recognized that look because his gaze held the same kind of look. Only, in his case, it was all about him coming for her. The emotions he felt hit him sideways. Odd to think about caring for this woman when he hadn't cared for anyone after all these years.

As he looked out the window of his vehicle, he could see the day waning away, but he'd gotten a lot done so far. He'd get back to his motel and stay at it. He didn't have a clue when his people would contact him again. At least he had a good start on solving this case. Now, if only he could force the cops to drag in Stanley, who owned the car on the ferry, for questioning. Would Stanley say anything though? Not likely. He probably has been well paid for his part in this.

And Tom Paine? The cops needed to talk to him too, but Tom wasn't any mastermind. That much was for sure. Yet he had the connection to Scion Labs, Amanda's employer. So was Tom getting paid too, directly from his previous employer to screw over his current employer, meaning, his own grandmother and grandfather? *Family*, ain't they just grand at times?

Well, at least Kerrick knew where to find Tom tomorrow. At work.

Kerrick drove back to the motel, stopping to pick up food. He ordered another burger and fries, hating that he was eating a lot of fast food but needing the sustenance, and parked outside the motel.

Back in his room, he quickly set up his laptop again and researched Stanley. What if, on his own, Kerrick could contact Stanley directly? Maybe scare the crap out of him to get him to talk? Kerrick searched online for a physical address or anything that would give him a location, but he found nothing. And, if Stanley no longer worked at the trucking company, what's the chance he would talk anyway? It's not like he could lose a job he didn't have anymore.

By now Jimmy, the nervous weasel, would have forewarned both Tom and Stanley. Sighing, Kerrick bet that Tom Paine would *not* be returning to work tomorrow.

It was well past business hours now and getting darker out and now thirty-one hours of captivity for Amanda. And that's why Kerrick needed to track down a few more of these people. He hated to lose all of the night to sleep, although he did have to catch some shut-eye to be able to do this job right, to divert any jet lag. So much information still had to be found, and Kerrick had absolutely no inkling where Amanda was being held.

What if Jimmy or Stanley or Tom didn't disengage the GPS on that lorry? Surely one of the three of them would have covered their asses. Still, after meeting two of them, Kerrick decided to see what information that GPS could give him.

He contemplated breaking into the trucking parking lot overnight and then wondered if he could hack into the computer system instead. He quickly opened his special chat window and ordered the GPS tracking info on the lorry. The answer was a single question mark.

He typed **Do it.**

He sat here and ate his burger and fries, wishing he'd picked up at least one coffee. When he was done, he tossed his garbage, grabbed himself a large glass of water, and drank that down. By the time he returned to his laptop, the chat window had a message waiting for him and a link. He quickly went into the link, and, sure enough, it provided the LoJack mileage data on lorry 714 to date. He went back to the day in question, and there it was—the path that the lorry had taken on Sunday.

Even with three guys involved in using a stolen lorry, not one had considered disengaging the LoJack on it. Wow, talk about cocky. Or just plain stupid. But while the LoJack gave Kerrick the total mileage traveled on that Sunday by the stolen lorry, it didn't tell him anything about the locations reached along that journey. And the mileage racked up that day indicated one hell of a trip. Like to Paris and back?

He went back to the chat window. **Get the map for Sunday's route from the LoJack company.**

Almost immediately, as if having already anticipated what he needed, another link popped up. And there he was, into the security system and checking the exact route the lorry had traveled. With that, he brought out his paper map, courtesy of the local airport—and always good to have on hand as a backup. He spread out the map on the bed with his laptop beside him. He quickly used a highlighter to mark off the lorry's route on his physical map.

As expected, it was a circuitous route. The lorry had traveled to France to kidnap Amanda from Scion Labs in Paris and had returned to England, obviously meeting up with the blue car on the French side of the ferry. And the two vehicles had crossed together, as confirmed on the ferry images. Why two vehicles? The only thing Kerrick could think of was the kidnappers feared the lorry would be searched before being allowed on the ferry.

For sure, a "sleeping" woman in the back of a lorry would raise eyebrows. Whereas a "sleeping" woman in the back seat of a car, obvious for all to see, didn't seem so suspicious.

Regardless, Tom and his hairy arm drove Stanley's car onto the ferry and then onto land in England, while the lorry driven by Stanley soon took the lead and headed into the Liverpool area. There, it had stopped at a couple spots—one Kerrick suspected was where the car had been loaded into the lorry. The lorry had driven another seventeen miles before it stopped again, dropping off Amanda, then had returned to the trucking company yard.

This last stop had likely been where the car had been removed, simply because of the way the lorry was parked away from the fence, like to secretly unload a car. But all that conjecture did not tell him where the car had gone afterward. He again typed into the chat box and asked if there was any sign of the blue car yet.

**No.**

**We need to find it.**

**On it.**

Of course they were on it. The car could be key to finding Stanley. But at least now he knew where the lorry had stopped, where the lorry might have dropped off Amanda. It was a run-down commercial area of town; Kerrick could get back into the traffic cams to find the car hopefully. Moving his laptop from the bed back to the table, he sat down, logged again into the traffic center, and searched through the feeds. He didn't have access to the main city of Liverpool, though he quickly asked the chat window for the login. It took a moment, and then he had another link. He was loving this. He seemed to have access to anything. Granted, he didn't have free *direct* access, but, if it was a reasonable request, so far he had been given whatever he needed.

Back in the traffic cams, at this one location where the lorry had stopped—at least as far as he could tell from this particular angle—was a large loading bay. And that would make sense. There would not likely be any cameras picking up the lorry, but, … if Kerrick was lucky … He sat here for the next several hours, fighting exhaustion and jet lag, skimming through the traffic feeds and looking for the car or the big lorry. Then his laptop dinged as the chat window provided another link. He clicked it to see a video camera feed of a big lorry backing up to a loading bay off to the side of some huge industrial building, its rear doors open. As he kept watching, the blue car reversed out of the lorry and drove away. He crowed in delight. **That's it.**

Instantly a thumbs-up emoticon appeared in the chat window.

He laughed. **So you do have a sense of humor. We need to track that car now.**

But, of course, they already were. It took another two minutes, and then his screen flashed. Frowning, he checked out what was coming—a feed recorded earlier, showing the route that the blue car had traveled. Unfortunately he never saw the driver. It could have been Stanley, since it was his car. Or it could have been Tom, since he was mainly driving the car that Sunday. Hell, both men could have been in the vehicle for all Kerrick could tell. That left Jimmy to return his lorry back to the overnight parking lot at the trucking company. So he was driving that third vehicle after all. Kerrick never tracked it very far, only seeing it a couple, three times. And then it disappeared—into the back of the lorry. Pretty brilliant for three stupid crooks.

"Interesting," he murmured as he quickly took notes. The car headed past a hospital, turned around into the back, but then, almost as if thinking it was in the wrong place, pulled back out again and headed away. He frowned at that. "What's the matter? This guy not know where he's going?"

He kept watching as the vehicle pulled ahead into another large medical complex with a huge but run down sign out front. There, it went into an underground loading area, where Kerrick couldn't see it anymore. Kerrick waited and watched but in Fast Forward mode. The vehicle came back out close to forty minutes later per the time stamp on the video. The thing is, this time, from what he could see of the driver, just his shirt-covered chest, it looked to be a different driver, a bigger guy. Kerrick zoomed in as the car took an incline and could see it was a larger man with a beard now.

"Damn it." He sent a screen shot to his people via the chat window. **Got a partial facial photo but try to match it.**

**Won't be easy. Only got his beard to go by, and the beard covers major facial markers needed to ID him.**

**Do your best.**

Kerrick frowned, wondering what had happened to the original driver—Tom? Stanley? Jimmy? Someone else?—and that's where the feed ended. He immediately dropped back into the chat box, asking for the rest of the feed. **We need to find that vehicle**, he added on his message.

He was given immediate access once more. He quickly searched and watched as the car was picked up by various traffic cameras on its route, and then finally he could see it off in the distance, heading toward a country pasture. Another vehicle was close behind it, with only a driver inside—and this car was *not* the third one used earlier as a diversion at Dover. These two vehicles got up to a bridge, and Kerrick lost the blue four-door there. He kept searching and waiting, but nothing else showed up again. Kerrick sighed. It was a blind spot in the cameras. But he did catch the other vehicle, a gray two-door, driving away, and this time two people were in the front seat. The picture was grainy, the car too far down the road. *Interesting …*

**That canal needs to be checked up at the bridge. Stanley's blue four-door car will be down there. Still, we could find the dead bodies of Stanley, Tom, and/or**

**Jimmy anywhere anytime now too. Let me know what you find.**

There was an acknowledgment on the chat window, and Kerrick was happy to have the help on that because Kerrick didn't have time. He checked his watch and realized it was almost midnight. He needed at least four hours of sleep a night, but that would have to come later. He closed the chat window, dropped the lid on his laptop, made his preparations quickly, gathering all he would need for his upcoming night maneuver, and had a hot shower.

# CHAPTER 6

T HE DARKNESS PLAYED with her senses. Amanda lived in
an unceasing cycle of dim light. She tried all the doors
in the hallway for her floor, deemed the basement as far as
she knew. Every door was locked. A knock and her whispered, "I'm here to get you out," didn't get any responses.
Only her door was unlocked. She quickly dashed to the far
side of this building, but she was in a corridor of more
locked doors. She opened one to find it was a closet. She
stepped inside, looking for anything to help her. She found a
pair of coveralls that she hastily pulled on over her dirty
clothes and an old hat. She stopped, looked around for a
weapon, finding instead a mop and also a bucket—not much
of for weapons. But both would give her a bit of cover.

She grabbed them and carried them out into the hall and
checked every one of the doors on each side of this hallway
and again found nothing unlocked and nobody responded to
her whisper at each door either. She headed back down the
third hallway, doing the same checks for each hallway for
each side of this building. There had to be a way to get out
of this damn place. She passed a double door and stopped.
She opened the door, relieved to find that it wasn't locked. It
led her to stairs heading up *and* stairs heading down. Her
heart pounded, worried that a ton of the bad guys were in
this building and that she wasn't the only kidnap victim

here.

*Up or down?*

She hesitated, but the little boy who spoke to her in Morse code was up one floor. So she bolted up the stairs, still carrying her mop and bucket as she headed to the next flight. She could see a small window showing the outside world, so this floor where the boy was held was at ground level. Which meant she had been incarcerated belowground, and yet, another floor was below hers too, given the up and down staircases she had just seen.

Where the hell was she? What was this place? It was dark outside, but her days and nights were all twisted up and turned around, so that she didn't know if this was dusk or dawn. She should have warned Brandon that she was coming, but there'd been no time. Neither could he likely tell her where he was located in this mausoleum. Still, she had a good idea where she had been, and he was directly above her.

She went into the first hallway on this floor and again found it empty, nobody responding from behind the locked doors. She didn't have a clue what all these rooms held. Around the corner was the next hallway on this floor and had almost no doors. She kept tracking the direction to where her room would be underneath. Why had she seen no workers here? Orderlies? Guards? For all she knew, this building was empty and deserted, except for its captives, with a crew coming once a day or every couple days to throw food and water at them.

She raced as fast as she could, using long strides to get down to what she thought would have been the equivalent of her room below. She stopped at the corner, considered how many doorways were to the left, then walked over by three and grabbed the knob and turned it. It opened. But the room itself was empty.

*Shit.* She stopped. She reorganized her thoughts, trying to figure out how many doors to the left down *her* hallway were there, but this was the corresponding room she was searching for on this level. She was sure of it. However, just in case the floors weren't quite exactly duplicates, she went one door to the left and opened it. It was also empty. Cursing, she went one door to the right, and it was locked. She tapped on the door, and there was a delay before she heard a responding tap. She then tapped a question in Morse code. *Is it you?*

The answer came back *Yes.*

She tried the door again, but it was locked. She could hear him pounding on the door. She waited until he stopped and then tapped *Stop. Be quiet. I have to find out how to open the door. I'll be back.*

And then she left. A matching closet should be down the little boy's hallway as well, if this floor was anything like her floor. There, she raced inside, looking for anything. Again she found nothing to use as a weapon. But there were more coveralls. She quickly checked inside the pockets of each pair, looking for keys that would unlock that door, but found nothing. Then she found the mother lode. A large key ring. Hanging on a hook on the wall.

She stared at it in joy but then realized it could take her an hour to figure out which one belongs to which door. And surely it was just keys to places that didn't matter, right? Because they wouldn't leave prisoners behind locked doors and also leave behind the keys displayed openly on a wall, would they?

Pulling out one of them, she smiled because it was a

master key. She headed back to the same room, and, just as she was about to put the key in the door, she heard voices. She immediately disappeared around the corner and returned to the closet. She rehung the keys on the wall but not before she took the master key. She tucked it into her pocket and disappeared, hiding behind the rack of coveralls.

The only way to make this work was if she tried to be as flat as she could with the coveralls hanging before her. She heard the voices come down the hallway, but they didn't open the door to the closet. She waited, knowing that, if they went one direction, they had to come back again.

But how long would they take? As she waited, she heard the footsteps again. This time they stopped at the door. Somebody opened the closet and said, "This is just the broom closet, in case we need something for spills or to clean up the blood. If it's a big job, we call in the cleaning crew."

She frowned at his tone and his wording, almost as if giving a tour to somebody on his first day at a new job. But the sound of cleaning up blood didn't make her feel any better. And, if it was bad, bringing in a cleaning crew? Yeah, she could imagine.

The voices continued, and she heard, "During the night, we clean out the chamber pots. It's gross. Every one of these rooms should have their own bathroom. If they were in the upstairs rooms, they do, but these downstairs rooms don't." Then the closet door was closed again, and she heard their footsteps getting farther and farther away.

She snorted silently. "Great," she muttered. "I get to be in one of the worst rooms. Doesn't that just suck?"

When she thought it was long enough, she slowly opened the closet door and stuck her head out. Saw no sign of anyone. She stepped into the hallway and raced back to

Brandon's door, hoping that the men hadn't taken the kid away. Using the master key, she quickly unlocked his door. A terrified pale-faced boy stood on the other side. "Brandon?" She opened her arms, and he raced into them. She quickly shut his door again and whispered, "We have to go now."

He wore just shorts and socks and a T-shirt. He held his shoes in his hands, almost as if he thought he could sneak out quieter without wearing them. She motioned for him to get those on fast. She looked around, thinking of anything else in that closet which would be of help to him. *That old jean jacket.* She held up a finger, raced back, quickly snagged it, and brought it to him, putting it around his shoulders. And then she led him back to the stairs. What she didn't know was how to get out of this building.

"Do you know where we're going?" Brandon asked in a loud whisper.

She shook her head. "No. I found stairs but no exit yet."

He nodded. "We need to find that first."

"Suggestions?" she asked, hating the idea of going down the hallway any farther. "That's where the men came from," she said, pointing. "I just about got caught by two of them."

His only response was to stare at her, and she could see the whites of his eyes and how his mouth was pinched tightly together.

She nodded, as if making a decision, then said, "The stairs have to go somewhere."

He stayed close to her as they headed to the stairwell.

There, she motioned up top and said, "Let's go up one more flight. I can see light there, and I know we're above-ground here, but we should check the next level anyway. Then decide on our next move."

They quickly made their way upstairs to what appeared

to be the main floor, and, sure enough, they found a door, with an alarm at the top. She hesitated, pointed at that bright red light, and said, "When the door opens, an alarm could go off."

"But we still need to open it," the boy said as he peered through the nearest window into the darkness. "Do you think there's any chance of getting away from here?"

"This *is* our chance," she said firmly. "If we don't get away on this attempt, we're in deep trouble. They'll lock us up, throw away the key, and then we won't even be given that little bit of food that we've had so far."

"What food?" he mumbled. "I could eat this jacket by now."

"Well, let's hope it doesn't come to that."

Just when she was about to take a deep breath and open the door, they heard voices again, and the door at the top of the stairs opened. They stared at each other in horror. She quickly grabbed him and pulled him back so they were out of view—as long as nobody came down the stairs—hoping that the new arrivals were going up instead.

The voices at the top of the stairs called out, "So do we need to show you the downstairs again too?"

That sent Amanda and Brandon silently scampering down to his floor. Again. Where they waited to see what the newcomers did next.

KERRICK HAD PARKED one-quarter mile away and hiked the rest of the distance to the GPS location where the lorry had unloaded the car, and hopefully Amanda too. Google Maps had ID'd the location as a huge sanitorium that had closed down and been left derelict. And yet, if it was derelict, this building shouldn't have been powered, and there was definitely power. He could see lights on inside. A few vehicles were parked around the building too. So obviously not derelict, no matter what Google told him.

He headed toward the side fence and jumped over it, just in case working cameras checked out people at the main entrance. If other people were held in here, then it was quite possible that the kidnappers had a very extensive security system. Kerrick hoped not but knew he would do what he could to not trigger any alarms. "Hang on, Amanda," he whispered. "I'm coming."

Once he got to the building, he quickly geared up, shaking his head at the surprising haul hidden in his car. Bolstered to have everything he needed, he walked around, looking at the six stories rising above, potentially a seventh or a penthouse that he couldn't quite see. He had no idea how many stories deep it went. But, depending on how many rooms filled each floor, there could be hundreds of patients held here. There was no business sign, no welcoming entrance, and not even a set of double doors that evidenced any kind of regular interaction with people. And yet, this place appeared operational. He crept alongside the building, noting the exits. Two were at the back, with a fire exit on the other side.

Kerrick also found a shipping bay for deliveries on the right-hand side. The driveway dipped into a floor-to-ceiling gated area and went down where a series of raised docks were for unloading at the same level as the lorries. All in all, pretty standard stuff for a commercial building. But the double doors on the bays looked old, as if they probably wouldn't even open. At least, not easily. And that was something else to consider.

If that's where the lorry had driven, which to the best of Kerrick's knowledge it was, why here? Why not just park in the front, unload the woman, and take her in that way? Unless it was just easier down there. It's also possible no cameras were down there to ID the woman. Although the street cams had caught sight of the lorry as it backed up here.

With that thought in mind, he crept his way down the back of the building in the darkness, dressed fully in black, his face blacked out too, and checked for an unsecured entryway, finding an unlocked side door. He opened that and stepped inside. He wore night-vision goggles, which made it easier to see anything. He moved slowly, getting his bearings on the inside of the building.

While the bay door area was for trucks to drive into the lower levels of the building, Kerrick noticed the downward slope of this more pedestrian area, diving deeper into the same area, he presumed.

One of the things about large and supposedly empty buildings like this was that it was often easy to lose track of your navigation sense. And that's something he couldn't afford to do. He kept on moving quietly through the floor. Boxes were off to one side, which he noted without investigating them further, but then farther along he found large pallets. He checked to see it was foodstuffs, and that meant people lived here, so they had to feed them. And they were feeding lots of people because there were multiple pallets.

He kept on moving, but he took photos as he went. He still saw no signs of anyone. It was a small operation based solely on how few cars were here, but he had already taken images of each of the vehicles parked out front—two lorries, a car, and an SUV. He did a complete search of this floor and counted how long that took. Twelve minutes. Realizing how long it would take to check every floor—even without opening every door to every patient room—he had to pick up his speed. But it was just him out here and no backup. He didn't like that part at all. His phone vibrated at his hip, and he pulled back into a far corner and checked it.

**Are you in?**

He tapped the phone twice for a *yes*.

**Backup is on its way.**

He smiled at that. **Who?**

**Friend.**

He stared at that word, but no further messages came. He pocketed his phone and went up one level to get a bird's-eye view. He located a newly installed elevator at one corner and three sets of stairs at the remaining three corners. He was still in the basement area of the building. After taking one more set of stairs, he could look out the nearby window and see the ground below.

Just as he went to the front of the building, passing more windows, he caught sight of somebody dressed in black, skirting around to the far side. He immediately tracked the newcomer to the back wall and then waited for the door to open. Just as it did, it seemed somebody instinctively knew Kerrick waited here. So, he tapped out his name in Morse code. He froze, and then, on the other side of the door, someone tapped out an affirmative *Yes*.

And then he asked, *Who the hell are you?*

*Griffin.*

Kerrick opened the door and flashed his light in the man's face. Eyes bright and deep emerald green stared back at him. They were twinkling. Kerrick reached out a hand, and Griffin caught it and squeezed hard. Kerrick didn't have time for explanations or questions, but he pulled his buddy in and shut the door tight. In a low whisper, Kerrick asked, "Are you up to speed?"

Griffin nodded. "Have checked out the grounds. All clear. But doubt it will stay that way."

Kerrick nodded and stepped through to the stairwell and said, "Down here first."

But Griffin pulled him back and pointed down.

Kerrick couldn't see anything.

By his ear, Griffin whispered, "Somebody's on the landing below us."

"Got it."

He stepped off to the side to peer down the stairwell, seeing two bodies pressed tight against the stairwell below. So, they heard him coming? That was just too damn bad. If they got in his way, he would take them out. But … one was small, in baggy coveralls. The other smaller. He held up a warning hand to Griffin, who joined him at his side, and they studied the two in shock. They looked at each other, and then, in a sudden move, Kerrick, using the railings, jumped up to the landing below in two moves, his weapon up tight against the taller of the two people frozen in front of him. And damn if that same clear and directed gaze from one of his photos didn't shine back at him.

"Who are you?" she snarled. Even with his gun poking her in the ribs, she raised her fists as if to clock him.

He quickly grabbed her hand, twisted it around her back, and pulled her tight against him, so she couldn't hit him. The child beside her immediately punched and kicked at Kerrick, but Griffin grabbed him and wrapped him up tight.

Kerrick whispered in the woman's ear, "Amanda?"

She froze, then slowly nodded.

"Good," he said. "You're the one we came for."

"But Brandon comes too," she was quick to demand.

With her in his arms, Kerrick raced back to the door where Griffin had entered. With both captives safely in their custody, they stepped outside into the cool night air. Kerrick whispered, "Don't make a sound. Don't make a move. Not until we tell you."

"How do I know whose side you're on?" she asked in an angry whisper.

He could see the fear in her gaze and also her determination to not let that stop her. But, as she stared into his eyes, she seemed to relax a bit. He smiled and said, "Well, I have a code word for you. Would that make you feel better?"

She frowned and said, "I don't know any code word."

"And why is it that you do cancer research?"

She stared at him, shook her head, and he whispered, "Because of your friend Alice."

She sagged against him, and he picked her up and carried her off into the night.

# CHAPTER 7

A MANDA DIDN'T KNOW if she should trust this stranger or not, but the fact was, she was outside her prison and breathing fresh air again. That was the best feeling ever. She held Brandon close in her arms. The poor kid was terrified. He had his arms wrapped tight around her waist, as they both stared up at the men with darkened faces. The men motioned them to move with them quietly.

Just as they headed down the path toward the front of the building, several vehicles pulled in, lights blazing. The two men grabbed her and Brandon and pulled them back behind the building.

She could hear one man swear under his breath. She looked around the property, but the fences were high and would be hard to cross. "Maybe we should go back inside," she whispered.

"Or maybe not," the other man said, his voice low. "If they're coming inside, we want to make sure that we're not caught in there. As soon as they go in the building, we need to get away from here."

"I don't know if there's any way out the back," Amanda stated. "Do you guys know?"

The second man looked over at the first and said, "Kerrick?

So that was his name. It's not like they had had time for

introductions.

Kerrick shook his head. "I didn't see anything. It's this fence all the way around."

The first man nodded. "Makes perfect sense. They shepherd people in, so they only have one direction to go."

"Like cattle," she supplied calmly. She waited to see if the footsteps sounded closer to them. But—other than being flat and tight against the building with the two men both ready and armed—there was just complete silence. Then shortly thereafter she heard car doors closing and lots of laughter from the people walking into the building that angered her more than anything.

They thought this was funny? They thought this was a good thing that she and this poor child and how many others had been imprisoned, freezing, day in and day out, surviving on moldy food and using piss pots instead of toilets? Just the audacity of these people made her so angry. She could feel the tremors running up and down her thin frame. And maybe Kerrick noticed too because he gripped her shoulder firmly and whispered, "Stand steady."

She just glared at him. He flashed a smile in her direction, but she didn't move. The second man leaned forward, ever-so-slightly, and held out three fingers and then dropped one. She waited, wondering what would happen when he dropped the other one. He dropped the second one, and Kerrick whispered, "As soon as he signals it, we'll run. Be ready."

"Great," she muttered, "but where?"

"We'll stay to the right and go through that open gate."

"A getaway vehicle would be better," Brandon muttered against her waist.

She felt more than saw a chuckle come from Kerrick. He

patted Brandon on the shoulder and then reached out a hand, grabbing both of theirs when the second man dropped his final finger. They bolted as fast and as silently as they could, racing along the fence on the right-hand side to the double gates that stood open. Then they were through. She wanted to scream in victory when she hit the other side, but the men weren't giving her a chance to catch her breath, and she knew that they were a hell of a long way from being out of danger.

Just when she thought that maybe they'd cleared the danger zone, they heard voices shouting behind them. With her breath coming in gasps and her chest burning, they raced faster. She thought they were heading for a road, but instead they pulled them into another building, and then they stopped, pressing up tight against another wall. She closed her eyes and tried to calm down her breathing. But each breath rasped out, sounding like a huge cacophony of noise that people miles away would hear.

Brandon looked over at Kerrick and said, "Please tell me that you have a car or a truck to take us away."

Kerrick smiled at him and said, "Yes, but we don't want to be seen getting into it because then they'll follow us too easily."

Brandon smiled for the first time. "Good. If they try to take me a second time, I'll make them pay."

Amanda gave him a quick hug, then said, "The bad guys aren't taking us anywhere again. You and I have both had enough of that crowd."

She could feel the shiver of fear run over him, and she realized just how terrifying an event this must have been for the young boy. It had been bad enough for her. She couldn't imagine how he felt. He was only ten. The machinations of these evil and greedy people were not something any child should be exposed to. Not like this.

They waited again in complete silence. The trouble was her heart just kept pounding against her rib cage. The adrenaline still coursing through her bloodstream kept her revved up, unable to calm down. She could feel her blood pounding at her temples. Her breathing rasped hard in her dry throat from the mad dash. It was all she could do to get her breath under control, just in case she had to run again. It wasn't something she wanted to think about, but she would run until she dropped if it meant avoiding that nightmare.

JUST THEN THE second man stepped forward and farther away from them.

Kerrick called out in a low, urgent voice, "Careful, Griffin."

Griffin? Neither were names that she recognized, yet both were strong, warrior-type names. She appreciated that they were here with her and Brandon. She couldn't imagine escaping on her own, although she'd done well enough before these men had found her and Brandon. She'd gotten them out of their locked cells. These men had helped get them out of the building, but she couldn't put her trust in them too far. For all she knew, they wanted something else from them. How devastating would that be? She studied Kerrick's face, looking for any signs of deceit or betrayal, but it wasn't that easy. It was dark outside, and, short of staring into his eyes again, there was no way to know.

Griffin made a hand motion, and they crept forward. She heard people running, probably searching the grounds all around them for their escapees. So far, nobody had come onto this property.

"How did you know this building was empty?" she asked.

"I scoped it out earlier on a satellite feed," Kerrick said. "Griffin came out earlier this evening too. I knew we could get in this door because I'm the one who unlocked it."

She smiled. "Glad to hear that. It would help if you locked it now though, and then they couldn't get back in again."

"It's already done," he said.

And, realizing that the men seemed to have this well in hand, Amanda sagged against the wall and groaned lightly.

Immediately Brandon turned to look up at her. "Are you okay?" he asked anxiously. Then he spun to look at the other man. "She hasn't had much food or water for the last couple days, by my count of her captivity. She can't do much more of this."

She had some questions for this special little boy, but they would have to wait. Meanwhile she reached out a gentle hand and patted his shoulder. "I'll be fine. Remember how you haven't had any food or water either. Which may have been the better option, as mine were drugged."

"Just stay close," Kerrick said. "And stay silent. We'll get you where you need to go."

"That better be to a shower, a buffet table, and a hot bed," she said and then added, "And communication with the outside world."

"We'll be your outside communication for a while," Kerrick said.

"Are you turning us over to the police?"

He shook his head. "We're not sure the police even

know you're missing."

She stared at him in shock. "What?"

He nodded.

"But surely my father would have contacted them."

"He contacted our group instead," Kerrick said quietly. "And thank God that he did."

"He would do that," she murmured. "He's got connections I can't even begin to guess at."

Just then Griffin made a sound. Immediately Kerrick placed a finger on her lips. She stared at him wordlessly. Her mind was still trying to comprehend the situation. So, no law enforcement, which meant her father didn't trust the police. So, those connections he had, who she didn't know about, he had thought that this was the time to call on them? She shook her head.

All she wanted to do with her life was to cure cancer and to help save women like her best friend. And yet, men like these were out there who did this with their lives instead. It was almost too much to imagine what a life of darkness they led. A life of danger. A life of walking and living in the shadows. Did they ever come out for light? Did they have a normal life? Did they have wives and kids? Did they mow the lawn on Sunday and sit in the backyard and have a beer with a barbecue?

They didn't seem the type, but then what did she know? This was their work persona. It's what they did on their off time that had her curious. Just then they were moved gently to another location within the same building. And that didn't seem like a good idea to her.

She looked over and opened her mouth, but Kerrick gave a sharp shake of his head. Immediately she shut up again. At the back of the building, they stepped outside and moved across the property and around another building. She didn't know what was going on, and she had lost track of where they were as they wove between buildings, back and forth and around. And then, all of a sudden, Griffin was gone. She gripped Kerrick's hand and whispered in a low but urgent voice, "We have to wait for him."

Kerrick looked at her, squeezed her fingers, and said gently, "He's gone to get the car."

She stared up at him blankly, then looked around. "Oh."

"It'll be fine. Just give us a minute to get you into the wheels, and we can get away from here."

She looked over at Brandon to see his huge eyes shining in the darkness. He was tired and exhausted and famished, but also an element of excitement was evident in his expression. This was a story to tell whatever friends he had back home. These superheroes had dashed in the middle of the night to save them. She knew her own role in Brandon's tale was probably as the lost dumb blonde. That filled her with amusement rather than disappointment.

She was okay with whatever version he had to tell to get himself to move forward on this one. She didn't even know what she would say herself except she wanted to block it all out. But how was she supposed to do that when Hinkleman was her boss? Who was *she* supposed to tell this tale to?

Hinkleman was one of the shareholders who were part of the board of directors for her employer, Scion Labs. Hinkleman was highly regarded in his field. Or had been decades ago. And only by people who didn't deal with him day to day. Among those at Scion, Hinkleman was more feared than revered. She had seen him totally lose it, and it wasn't fun to watch. He was more of a bully and a blowhard in her opinion—probably who he truly was. He had been even more volatile lately. But he was unpredictable at best. She had just kept her head down at work, happy to have this huge lab facility at her disposal, to be paid to do what she loved and would have pursued regardless, what she felt was her purpose.

But Hinkleman had been here at this facility, knowing she was locked up like a prisoner. And he had hit her because her data was corrupt, when in reality he just couldn't read it. She shook her head at that. Frowning, she wondered how deep or how high this corruption went within the ranks of Scion. She, as a part owner too, as a major shareholder, felt partly responsible for cleaning up this mess. Why wasn't there any internal oversight as to Hinkleman within Scion? Surely there had been signs … and not just as to the verbal abuse of his researchers.

She desperately wanted to get back to her office and to see what had happened to her research, but she was a long way from doing that. Not to mention the fact that, if the company hadn't called about her absence from work, maybe they were in on this whole scheme too. Maybe it wasn't as great a company to work for as she had always thought. Maybe Hinkleman was just one of many on the board who was involved. Those were more thoughts to send shivers down her body. With her whole world collapsing around her, she could hear sounds of a vehicle coming closer. She stiffened and stared up in a panic at Kerrick.

He smiled and said, "It's Griffin."

She took a deep breath and let it out very slowly, then nodded.

KERRICK WAITED AS the vehicle pulled up within ten feet of them. It didn't have its headlights on, but the back door opened, and he quickly ushered them toward the car. They were placed in the back seat, and Kerrick took the front passenger seat, and, just as silently, the vehicle pulled forward and headed away from where she and Brandon had been prisoners.

"Not exactly a textbook escape," Kerrick said to Griffin as he sent a message to have the rental picked up. He might need more of the goodies that were still there too.

"Wasn't far off though," he said with a big smile. "Now to make sure we get a couple hundred miles away from these guys."

"We have to go back though," Brandon said.

Kerrick turned to look at him in surprise.

"It wasn't just us there," Brandon explained. "There are other prisoners."

"Did you see other people?"

He nodded. "When I first came in, I saw two others, a man and an older woman, but they were sleeping."

At the *sleeping* comment, Kerrick and Griffin exchanged hard glances.

"Were they on beds?" Griffin asked.

Brandon nodded. "Yes, like those hospital and ambulance gurneys. They were bringing them into the center."

"Did you recognize who they were?"

He shook his head. "No. The guards said something about Cynthia and Peter."

"And you think they were from the same family maybe?" Kerrick asked.

"The guards didn't mention that," Brandon said. "Adults always talk around kids. They think we don't hear anything."

Kerrick chuckled. "Well, they were wrong in your case. Anything else you can tell me?"

"The ambulance number was 41058," he said immediately.

Griffin stared at him in surprise. "Did you recognize the drivers or the men who were pushing the gurneys or anybody who was involved in kidnapping you?"

Kerrick wondered at what the kid could have seen, but, when Brandon started to talk, Kerrick quickly pulled out his phone and hit Record because it seemed Brandon had an incredible sense of recall. Whether it was his imagination or not was too early to tell, but he gave everything about the two guards, from the color of each guy's hair to the type of shoes each wore. Kerrick and Griffin exchanged hard glances as they listened to Brandon. When he finally ran down, Kerrick said, "Well, that's an awful lot of detail. I hadn't expected that much."

"Photographic memory," Brandon said quietly. "Most people laugh at me for it."

"We're not laughing," Griffin said. "We're ecstatic. Because you've given us lots of information, and hopefully we can use that information to help solve this."

Kerrick heard Amanda asking Brandon, "Do you have any memories of when you were locked up? Who came to see you? Who brought you food? What was in your room? Maybe it was different than what I went through."

Brandon shrugged and said, "It was four walls, a floor, and a ceiling. All appeared to be concrete."

And then he went into the same detail that he had spoken of before, describing the type of rotten food—which he refused to eat for the most part suspecting drugs but was smart enough to mash up and add to his chamber pot—who had brought in the food, how they were dressed, whether they had keys, and what kind of weapons they had.

Kerrick was stunned. "Is there any reason to suspect that your photographic memory is something that they know about?"

"I don't know how they would," he said.

"Does your father brag about it?" Amanda asked.

"My father thinks I'm a freak," Brandon said, his voice calm, like he was used to saying that a lot.

"You were smart enough to know Morse code and to use it, so I highly doubt that," Amanda rushed to reassure him.

But Kerrick had seen a lot of fathers who were assholes, so he wasn't so sure.

Brandon immediately said, "I don't mind. My father's kind of weird too."

"In what way?"

"He sells body parts," he said.

"As in organ-donor body parts?" Amanda asked.

There was silence first, and then Brandon, his voice very small, said, "Something like that."

Kerrick's heart hardened. If Brandon's father dealt in the black market for body parts, that put these kidnappers into a whole different level of criminal activity here. "Do you think that's why you were kidnapped?"

"Part of it, I'm sure," he said. "But it could be any number of things."

"Well, I'm interested in hearing your theories," Kerrick said, struggling to believe he was talking to a ten-year-old.

"Well, there's my dad's business," he said. "Plus, I'm one of those students who everybody loves to hate."

"With a memory like that, I'm sure you get straight As

all the time, don't you?" Griffin asked, looking at Brandon in the rearview mirror but smiling at him in a friendly and best-buddy way.

Brandon nodded. "Yes. I get very little wrong. And that makes everybody upset, including the teachers."

"They should be happy you're a star pupil."

He just shrugged and stared out the window. "Still makes me a freak. In the world, nobody likes freaks."

Amanda gripped his fingers and said, "I understand. But it gets better as you get older. I know. So, freak or not, I like you anyway."

Brandon chuckled at that. He turned to look at her and said, "Not many women know Morse code."

He was blissfully unaware of how sexist his comment came across. Whether it was his own upbringing or his limited experience, Amanda didn't know, but he'd completely slapped Amanda into a category of potentially being a dumb blonde. She just laughed, her voice soft and mellow as it floated through the vehicle, showing no signs of the strain of the last couple days. Low, melodic, and almost mesmerizing.

Kerrick struggled to keep all the details of her separated in his mind as the information flowed through the car. He was grateful he had his phone on Record because so much was discussed right now. It was hard for him to keep track of it all.

"I'm not a dumb blonde," she said gaily. "I'm not quite in the genius category as you are, Brandon, but …"

"*Amanda?*" Brandon said, his voice raising, as if something suddenly clicked into place. "*Amanda Berg?*"

"Yes," she said. In the review mirror, Kerrick could see her staring at Brandon in surprise. "What did you remember about me?"

"You're a Mensa, aren't you?"

She studied him carefully. And then she nodded, a grin spreading across her face. "I am, and so are you, *Brandon Coleman*. Aren't you?"

He gave her a big flash and a white smile. "Absolutely." He reached out of hand and said, "Pleased to meet you. You're more my kind than I thought."

While the two in the back seat carried on a quite animated conversation, Kerrick brought up a completely new point. He glanced over at Griffin and muttered, "What's another reason why the kidnappers would be collecting brains?"

"None I want to think about," Griffin said. "Particularly after somebody who provides body parts seems to be involved in this."

An edginess shifted down Kerrick's spine as he contemplated Griffin's answer. This was ugly. But it could get a whole lot uglier yet.

Kerrick directed Griffin to drive toward Kerrick's motel but had him bypass it and went on to another one he had seen not too far away, set off in the back corner of its property. It was little more than a dive, but it was a motel and had a second floor with direct outdoor access.

When he pulled their vehicle in front of the motel office, Griffin hopped out, leaving the car running, and headed inside. He came back less than two minutes later with keys, chuckling as he sat in the car again. "I didn't think the clerk would take my cash at first. Seems my burglar outfit scared him." Chuckling still, Griffin turned to face the two in the back seat. "Don't you like my pleasant and honest smiling face?"

Amanda groaned. "I'm sure you'd scare children and most adults with all those black marks on your face. But the clerk won't tell anyone that we're here, right?"

Griffin shook his head. "I made sure of that. He'll keep our secret to his grave."

Amanda's eyebrows rose as she looked at Brandon. "Good thing he's on our side, right?"

Now Brandon giggled too.

Griffin drove them around back, parking their vehicle between two huge SUVs, basically hiding it in plain sight. The two men quickly escorted their guests up to the second floor and into the double rooms that shared an interconnecting door. Griffin locked one front door, crossed over to the other room to the join the rest of them, and said, "I'll be back in a little bit."

"Don't you want to take the paint off your face first?" Brandon asked.

Griffin gave him a white-toothed smile and said, "Nope, not for this job." And he disappeared into the darkness of the early morning hours.

Kerrick motioned at the double beds in this room and said, "If you guys need to sleep ..."

"We need to eat, to drink, and I need a shower," Amanda announced.

Kerrick smiled and said, "Your bathroom's right there. Food's coming."

When Amanda took off for the bathroom, he pulled out his laptop and sat down.

Immediately Brandon hopped up at the kitchenette table across from him and said, "I really need to use your laptop."

"Why is that?" Kerrick asked, still struggling with the wise man inside the boy's body.

"To tell my dad that I'm safe."

Kerrick was busy on the chat page, letting his cyberteam know their latest location and that they had rescued Amanda and a kid but also warning his contact person that a lot more people were potentially being held in the same building. "Let me have my people do that, so nobody can trace our call. Is that okay with you?"

Brandon nodded.

"But I need to give them a quick update first, okay?"

Brandon nodded his head again, patiently waiting on Kerrick.

Kerrick wrote a short rundown and then uploaded the video and the audio tape that he had taken on his phone, mostly the ton of details that Brandon had handed over. It would be great if Kerrick's *people* could pull that together and maybe dredge up some matches to Brandon's descriptions via facial recognition software.

"You'll get to speak to your dad directly after we catch some of these bad guys, okay?" He nodded at Brandon, who seemed to understand, and asked, "Do you remember any names?"

Brandon blinked and, almost like a film reel rolling, started spouting names.

"I meant names from being kidnapped."

Brandon just gave him a droll look before spouting those in a fast string.

When he ran out of names, Kerrick made him repeat them, while checking his handwritten list and realizing he'd caught all but two of them. He sent that list off to his contact also, surprised to see Amanda joining them so soon. Her hair was dry, so she hadn't had her shower yet. "And you're both in the Mensa club, right?" He looked over at

Amanda and then back at Brandon. They both nodded. "Is there a special ranking system in the club?"

"Just our IQ level," Brandon said. "People like me love to be ranked. But, if you're not at the top, nobody wants to be ranked."

Kerrick chuckled at that. "Well, when you're the best of the best, nobody wants to know that they're the worst of the best."

Brandon laughed with the lightheartedness that a ten-year-old could.

Kerrick glanced at Amanda to see a wry look on her face. "Is it rude of me to ask, but is there a major difference between your IQs?"

She shrugged. "I don't know."

Brandon immediately popped up and said, "I'm 175."

She laughed. "Well, his IQ is higher than mine by one point."

"Is that enough to make a difference?"

She shrugged. "Not for me, no."

"Not enough, no," Brandon said.

"Did any of the people," Kerrick said, talking slowly, "and think about this now, were any of the people who you saw involved in this kidnapping mess, are their names associated with the Mensa group?"

Brandon's eyebrows shot up, and he sat back. "Interesting theory."

"But one we need to consider," Amanda said. "In my case, it was Dr. Hinkleman. In my opinion, he only joined Mensa for the public attention, for more accolades. But he was not actively engaged with the other members as far as I could see."

Kerrick turned to look at her in shock. "You know who

kidnapped you?"

"I don't know the men who took me off the street. I was grabbed by two men, and a hood was thrown over my head. Then I was tossed into the back of a lorry, alone. They remained on the street. The lorry drove off almost faster than my kidnappers could close the rear door. Then I heard the driver and his passenger talking at some point. So I counted four different men involved in my kidnapping.

"So the driver and a passenger were already inside the lorry. I didn't recognize their voices. So no idea who those men were either. I don't remember anything else until I woke up in this dark room, like a jail cell, and then yesterday, the day before, whenever"—she waved her hand as if she'd lost track of time—"when the guards came in, Dr. Hinkleman came in too."

"Interesting. So Hinkleman had no problem letting you see his face, correct?"

"He was my boss, supervised my work. My cancer research," she said slowly. "And when he came back a second time to see me in my cell, he was angry. He said something was wrong with my data."

"Was there?" Kerrick asked.

Brandon snorted. "Only that the others probably couldn't read it, right?"

Amanda gave a small shrug. "Potentially, yes."

# CHAPTER 8

AMANDA DIDN'T KNOW how to explain it but tried. "When I do my work, I must always consider theft issues, and people like to question your results and to test you, even when you haven't had a chance to finish your own experiments. So I've gotten into the habit of writing in a short form when doing theorems, doing that right from college. It's faster for me, and other people can't read it."

"So, when your boss said your data didn't work, was it because he couldn't read your shorthand?"

"It's possible," she said slowly. "But he did say that one of my coworkers had been working with my research. And, if it was somebody who I work with closely, they would have known ahead of time about my shorthand."

"Meaning, they should have been able to read it."

She shrugged and sat down on the third chair at the table. "Potentially. I don't know how hard it is for others to read. How long until we get food?" she asked, holding out her hand, palm up. She stared at her fingers, a little worried because they shook so bad.

"It's coming," he said, noting her concerned expression and her visibly shaking hand. "You should be eating within twenty minutes."

She nodded and said, "That'll be fine."

Brandon quickly reached out, grabbed one of her hands,

and held it in his. "Do you have blood sugar problems?"

"Only when I've been starved," she said, joking.

"Right. I thought my stomach would eat itself," he complained. "Don't they know how much food a ten-year-old needs?"

"Apparently not," she said, "or they didn't care."

"They didn't care," he said. He stared out the window, even though it was completely closed off with the blinds, his face glum. "I think that's the story of my life."

"What? That nobody cares?" Amanda asked.

"I think my father only kept me around because of what I could do for him."

Kerrick leaned forward suddenly. "Maybe you should tell me what you do for him?"

"Run probabilities, analyze the company data, and figure out where he'll make more money," he said. "It's pretty simple. He doesn't run a very complicated business, so it's not like I need a whole lot of financial education for his purposes."

Amanda smiled. "But so many people don't know how much we do understand and how much we don't, once we're labeled as a Mensa. It's expected that we know the velocity for traveling to the moon and what speed we need to lower to and how many feet off the surface."

He looked at her in surprise and nodded. "You *do* understand."

"Absolutely," she said as she leaned forward with a smile at the corner of her lips. "When I first started working at the lab, and they found out that I was a Mensa, people would ask me all kinds of questions, almost all to test my knowledge. But they were stupid questions, like, *Do you know how many skin cells are on an armadillo?*"

Brandon snorted at that. "You know what? I can't imagine the animal would sit still long enough for us to count, but we'd be talking minuscule amounts. Skin cells are sloughed off every twenty-four-hour period, so you'd be forever dealing with the fact that some of the skin cells would be falling off, and some would be ready to peel off. So, are they talking about the skin cells underneath *and* the skin cells that are in progress of being dumped?"

She nodded. "Exactly." She glanced up to see Kerrick frowning at her. She smiled and said, "Don't worry about it."

But his gaze darkened, and he shook his head. "It's amazing for those of us who don't have your brains to see just how much ability and smarts you guys have."

"Which is why I wanted to direct mine into cancer research," she said. "Particularly breast cancer. But then you already know that."

"I do," Kerrick said, "and I'm sorry for the loss of your friend."

She acknowledged his statement with a gentle nod of her head. "It was a very difficult time." She glanced over at Brandon suddenly and asked, "Where's your mother?"

His shoulders sagged, and he shook his head. Kerrick picked up the conversation. "Do you remember her at all?"

He shook his head again.

"Sorry, dude."

Brandon just shrugged. Amanda reached over and gripped his fingers. "It's tough, but it's something we end up living through."

"Exactly."

Just then a car door slammed outside.

She gasped, and her fingers started to shake. Brandon

gripped her hand tightly as they stared at each other in fear. Kerrick stood and peered through the blinds. "Dinner's here. Or whatever you want to call a meal at four in the morning." He got up, walked through the adjoining room, then stopped, and looked at them. "Do not *for any reason* open any door, do you hear me?"

They both nodded. She watched as he disappeared into the adjoining room, leaving the adjoining door slightly ajar, and then opened its outside door. She could hear him conversing with somebody, and she thought it was Griffin. She slowly relaxed. "It's okay," she said to Brandon.

When Kerrick returned with a large bag in each hand, she was surprised to find him alone. "Did you order delivery or something?"

"Or something," he said, deliberately not letting her know anything.

There had been a lot of secrecy between her and him. She really wanted to get some answers, but it was hardly the time or place. And she didn't know how much was necessary for Brandon to know. That massive brain of his was already churning through the details and trying to figure out this mess. It might be a good thing for him to face this head-on or for him to solve this all by himself even, but, at the same time, she wasn't sure he needed to know much more about evil human nature at this point.

Then the smell coming from the bags hit her, and she groaned. "Is that Chinese food?" she asked.

"We have Chinese food, fried chicken, and burgers," he said. "I didn't know what you wanted, so I ordered up a bunch of all of it."

Brandon gave a yelp of joy and raced toward the second bag. "Burgers? With fries?"

"Yes, but if you wanted anything special," he warned, "you won't be happy because I ordered straight off the basic menu."

"It's not the time to be worrying about specials right now," Brandon said. "That can wait until tomorrow."

"And what kind of special things do you prefer?"

"I hate pickles," he said. "Only drink one kind of pop. Chips have to be rippled and plain."

"Well," Kerrick said, "we don't have any chips nor do we have any pop. You can take the pickle off your burger." He quickly filled the table with food and handed a burger to each of them.

Amanda looked at hers and passed it over to Brandon and said, "You can have them both."

He turned toward her, frowned, and said, "You have to eat too."

She nodded. "I do, but I'll have my vegetables first."

He wrinkled up his nose at her as if to say, *Why on earth would anybody want vegetables?*

She laughed and said, "You'll understand this a little better as you get older."

He shook his head. "Hard to understand that theory. Vegetables are nasty at any age." His face wrinkling, he watched as she pulled out multiple boxes and containers of Chinese food and chopsticks.

She opened the containers, checked inside, grabbed the chopsticks, looked around, and asked, "Are there any dishes here?"

Kerrick got up to check the little kitchenette and shook his head. "Can you eat out of the container?"

When he turned around, she smiled, her mouth already full, and mumbled, "Absolutely."

She settled back and had a portion of each of the different dishes, everything from almond chicken to diced chicken to beef and broccoli as well as several noodle dishes too. Her stomach registered as full in no time, and she was scared to overload it after so many days of contaminated food and water. When she looked at Brandon, both his burgers were gone and so were the fries.

He eyed her Chinese food, slowly reaching out.

When she pointed out the box of fried chicken, his face lit up, and he reached in and grabbed a leg.

She smiled and had one for herself too. She looked over at Kerrick and asked, "Is this supposed to be food for you and Griffin too?"

"Griffin will bring more back," he said. "I'm waiting for coffee."

She moaned at that thought. "I would absolutely love a coffee. But now that the food is in me, I'm scared to put too much more in my stomach." Then she turned to Brandon. "Don't eat too much. It might come right back up again."

He nodded and said, "But I doubt it." And then he reached for another piece of chicken.

She got up, walked around, had a drink of water from one of the bottles that Kerrick had brought, and said, "Now I'll have that shower." She looked down at her clothes. "Unfortunately I have no clean clothes to change into."

"Not yet," Kerrick said. But he didn't give her any reassurances that clean clothes would be coming anytime soon or that she'd be heading back to her own apartment in the near future either.

But still, a shower would make a huge difference. She smiled, nodded, and said, "Don't get into any trouble while I'm gone, you guys."

KERRICK FACED BRANDON and said, "Now that your stomach's almost full, is there anything you can tell me about Amanda that would help us find out what was going on in her world?"

"She's doing cancer research. Her next step is to get approved for human trials," Brandon said as he reached for yet another piece of chicken.

*Human trials. Bingo.* He'd float some theories on that by Griffin. But right now he didn't want to focus any more on human body parts with Brandon. Kerrick was amazed at how much food that kid could put down. He might be ten years old, but he was eating for three grown men.

"So you didn't eat any of the food that they gave you?"

"Only enough to keep alive. Even if it was poisoned, in the amounts I ate, it was not enough to put me under." Brandon shook his head. "None of us have gotten much food at that place."

"Did they have trolleys outside? Did you see if the other patients were getting food trays at the same time?"

"No," Brandon said, "but the thing about being a kid is that they talk in front of me all the time because they don't think I have any smarts to understand."

"Gotcha," Kerrick said. "So, what did you overhear?"

"They were talking about Amanda. How one of the bosses was pissed right off. They didn't know if they could stop him from killing her."

"But they wanted to stop him from killing her?"

"He wanted her to go into the lab and to start working again. He wanted to keep her as a prisoner for a long time until she was done with her work."

"That's not nice," Kerrick said, frowning. In fact that was beyond ugly.

"There wasn't anything nice about those men," Brandon said.

Kerrick nodded. She could have been kept for years in that kind of a state. They would have been forced to give her food and water in order to have her brain function properly, but, if she couldn't recover her original notes or prove her theorems, they might have just thrown her out with the garbage the next time.

Brandon frowned and said, "I think they were talking about something else too. I wasn't sure though."

"Can you tell me what they said?"

"Something about multiple buyers and multiple deals for the same person."

"And did you have any idea what that meant?"

"Not really. Something about getting paid to do favors for more than one person at the time, but they were talking about Amanda."

"You heard her name mentioned?"

He nodded. "They talked about her a lot."

"How did you feel when you realized Amanda was in the room below you?"

"I wanted to tell her to run," he said. "To get away."

When Kerrick heard another sound outside, he peered once again into the darkness of the night.

But it was Brandon who said, "It's Griffin."

Kerrick glanced at him and asked, "How do you know?"

"I recognize his footsteps," he said candidly.

"You're really into this stuff, aren't you?"

Brandon nodded. "It's how I knew Morse code." Then he frowned and looked toward the bathroom. "How did she know about Morse code?"

"Because I think, like you, she has eclectic tastes and interests," Kerrick said. "Remember? She's a Mensa too."

Brandon nodded thoughtfully. "Most of the Mensas aren't even like me. I think there's something wrong with my brain. I think that's why I'm a Mensa. Not because I'm really smart but because there's something weird about my brain."

"I don't think so," Kerrick said, shaking his head. "You are a Mensa and, even if you didn't have that label, you're smart. That's the bottom line. Don't ever try to hide it. Just don't make a point of shoving it in everybody's faces."

Brandon chuckled. "I've been told that before too."

Kerrick could imagine. When a series of knocks came at the door to their adjoining room, he nodded and said, "I'll let Griffin in. You stay where you are, please."

Brandon nodded, and, as soon as Kerrick turned away and then glanced back, Brandon had already reached into the bucket of chicken for another piece. At this rate, they would need to buy the same food all over again. The kid was a bottomless pit.

Kerrick went through the connecting door, barely shutting it, and opened the front door of the other room for Griffin, who stepped in and handed him two more bags.

"I hope more of this is food," Kerrick said. "That kid's eating us out of house and home."

Griffin looked over at the adjoining door to see that nobody was there, and, in a lowered voice, he said, "There's been no call about the kid being missing. We tracked his father down. We know who he is, but he hasn't put out the word to anybody as far as we can tell."

"What's the chance that this is a punishment of sorts for the kid? Or maybe his father was just happy to get rid of him?"

"There are a lot easier ways to get rid of someone that are more permanent and more cost-effective," Griffin whispered. "His dad will never be Father of the Year material in my eyes. So, playing devil's advocate, he could just take him out back and deep-six him. Better than that, his dad might as well sell his body parts and get some money."

"Sad to say, just knowing that his dad didn't report Brandon as missing, I can see his dad doing the worst possible thing—that second theory you mentioned." Kerrick grimaced and shook his head. "Something weird is going on there."

"I know. It did occur to me that, letting me again play devil's advocate, what if the kid's a spy?"

At that, Kerrick's eyebrows shot up as he contemplated it. "Interesting theory."

"Maybe, but doesn't mean I'm wrong. We have to keep an eye on him."

"Agreed. It would be an interesting twist to the tale. What else did you find out?" He made his voice louder as they walked through the connecting door to the other room. Kerrick put down the bags on the table and then took the coffee cup holder from Griffin and put it on the table too.

Brandon looked with interest at the cups, but Kerrick shook his head and said, "You don't need any caffeine."

"No," he said. "I need sleep. And preferably a warm bed. And I suppose she'll make me take a shower too."

"When was the last time you had one?" Griffin asked.

Brandon just shrugged and said, "No clue."

"Well, there's your answer," Kerrick said.

Just then the bathroom door opened and a smiling pink-faced Amanda walked out in the same clothes but with a towel wrapped around her hair. Immediately she looked at Brandon and said, "Your turn."

He frowned at her, not moving.

She shook her head and pointed.

He groaned, but he got up obediently. Then, before really surrendering, he said, "Don't finish the chicken when I'm in there."

"I promise I'll save you *one* piece," Griffin said as he reached into the bucket and pulled out three for himself.

At that, Brandon raced into the bathroom. "I'll be superfast."

"Make sure you wash behind your ears," Amanda scolded. "And, if you come back out and that hair is not clean, I'll take you back in there myself." The door was slammed harder than necessary on her words.

She chuckled and said, "Boys will be boys." She walked over, looked at the food with interest, and then nodded and reached for a piece of chicken herself. "I think I'm full, and then, after a few minutes, I realize that I really want more food."

"That's fairly typical too," Kerrick said.

She waited a few minutes, with her head cocked, and he realized that, once the water could be heard running in the shower, she turned and said, "Okay. Now, what did you find out?"

Kerrick sighed, motioned at the nearest empty chair for her, and said, "There's no word at all about Brandon. Nobody's looking for him. His father hasn't called anybody, as far as we can tell."

She sat down while staring at him in horror, and then, with a lowered voice, she said, "Do you think he paid to keep him there?"

"But why?" Griffin asked her on a mouthful of fried chicken. "Why would he?"

She sat back and thought about it. "I guess there are cheaper ways to get rid of a child these days, particularly given Brandon's father's line of business."

Kerrick immediately nodded. He had his laptop up and was working away, his fingers clicking on the keyboard.

"So, what are we doing from here?"

"We'll hang low for the moment," Kerrick said, without looking up. "So get as much sleep as you possibly can. We'll stand watch in shifts, and then, hopefully by dawn, we'll have new plans."

"I don't know if I can go back to my apartment or my job," she said abruptly.

"Obviously we don't know everything about this," Griffin said, "but your boss is definitely involved. That puts the spotlight on the company, Scion Labs, and its people will know where you live. It's not even a possibility to consider going back to your office or to your home."

She sagged in place. "I need my laptop," she said quietly. "You have to understand. It's got my life's work on it."

"Your place has probably been cleaned out of anything useful. Just think about it. Your boss was after your work already. And, when they found what they had was corrupt, don't you think they would have immediately gone to your home office and took your electronics?"

"I had a laptop with me, when they kidnapped me," she said. "They probably thought it had my research work on it."

"And does it?"

She shook her head. "No, I ran a home server. It's hidden."

"Back to that *scared of somebody stealing your research?*"

She shrugged. "Maybe."

"Can you log in to your server remotely and download the information?"

She looked at his laptop, frowned, and said, "Maybe."

"Can you give me your router ID?"

Surprised, she nodded and said, "Well, I could, but what good would that do?"

"I could log in to your router and, therefore, into your network, if you've got the passwords memorized. And potentially we can access everything and download it to this laptop."

She frowned as she thought about it. "I have a lot of it on cloud storage but that last bit, I need to get from the server."

Brandon bounced out of the bathroom, already reaching for more chicken.

Amanda smiled. "Your hair is wet. Did you wash behind your ears?"

Brandon grimaced, immediately looking guilty.

"And did you wash all over, including your hair, with soap or shampoo?"

"Yes." At Amanda's questioning look, Brandon groaned. "May I eat more chicken before Griffin eats it all?"

At her nod, he ate like a starving kid.

Kerrick twisted around his laptop so she could see the screen and pointed her to the little chat window. "Type the router number in there." She did that, and he said, "Then, once you see your network pop up, type in your network password." She did, and, just like that, there were her files. She shuffled the laptop a little farther away from him and started moving material.

Kerrick didn't want to butt in when she was so obviously

trying to protect her stuff, but he said, "Unless you have a key, this laptop's not totally secure either."

She nodded. "I'm moving it to cloud storage, but I don't want my footsteps tracked."

He shrugged. "I can't guarantee that's possible right now."

She looked at him for a long hard moment and then quickly moved the laptop closer to her and glanced at Brandon.

Brandon moved his chair so it touched hers. He continued to eat, but he gave her a nod or a headshake as needed with each of her looks or a finger pointing to the screen.

Kerrick didn't know what she was doing as a workaround, but he suspected that the two great minds in this room would figure it out somehow.

When she and Brandon were done, she sat back with a pleasant smile and said, "At least now I have my material."

"And you still need your laptop?"

"Preferably. I'd like to get my laptop and my server from my place. But it is all hidden. So, short of the bad guys finding it—and I don't think they did, or they wouldn't have needed one of my assistants to read my research notes—so I don't think anybody looking casually will find it."

"What about guys like us?" Griffin said.

She gave him a fast frown and said, "I don't know. Depends on how well you look."

Kerrick was interested to see what she would consider to be a hard-to-find hiding spot like that. "If it's not a priority, I don't want to make the trip to France just yet," he said. "That'll just put both of you in more danger. But I can have your electronics picked up and kept somewhere safe."

"And I can get it back when I need it?"

He nodded. "Absolutely."

"Okay then. Let me know if your guys have trouble finding it."

Kerrick smirked but said, "I will, if needed."

She glanced at Brandon and then at Kerrick. "Do you have a safe house where Brandon and I can stay for a while?"

"We have a place," he said, wondering about that himself, now typing in the chat box to find Amanda's hidden electronics at her house and then to line up a safe house. "What about your father? What's your relationship with him?"

Her face softened, and the corners of her lips tilted. "We're very close," she said.

"So we'll get a message to him that you're safe," he said. "But I don't think you should have any direct contact with him until we know more."

She groaned. "Seriously?"

He nodded. "Because we don't know yet who else is involved."

"Well, as long as you pick up my ex-husband," she said, "you've got one-third of the equation."

"What's he got to do with this?"

"No clue," she said, "but Hinkleman told me three parties were interested in getting me out of the way."

"Who?"

"My father's enemy, my ex-husband, and then … Hinkleman himself?" She shrugged.

"That's what I assumed too."

# CHAPTER 9

IT HURT TO say that her ex-husband was involved. Amanda just didn't understand how or why. "He does make a good scapegoat," Amanda said. "Yet I'm not exactly sure I believe Hinkleman when he said my ex was involved."

"Why either way?"

"We signed the divorce papers five years ago, and he got nothing." She shrugged. "So him caring now doesn't make any sense."

"So he wouldn't be involved because you've already signed the divorce papers, but he would be involved because he got nothing?"

She nodded at him. "That's a good way to put it. It was a very bitter divorce, and we weren't married very long either."

"Why the divorce?"

"Because he didn't have any intention of being faithful, and I had absolutely no intention of being unfaithful while I was married. When I realized that we had such different philosophies as to what a true relationship was, I wasn't sticking around."

"So you initiated the divorce?"

She nodded. "Yes, and after only six months." She watched as he winced. She nodded. "Right. Six months and that's it."

"And he got nothing because the marriage was so short?" He nodded as if that made sense.

"He got nothing because of the prenuptial agreement I insisted he sign." There was a moment of silence as both men stared at her. "And why would I not?" she said. "It was important to me that he have no access or no benefit from control of my research, and, in some countries, material that you work on and discuss with your partner and/or research during a marriage can be something that he can claim as a part owner. I wouldn't allow that."

"Smart," he said. "There could be a tremendous amount of money involved in finding a cure for cancer."

"I already have a lot of money. It's a fallout of being a Mensa."

At that, Griffin snorted. "Are you saying all Mensas are wealthy?"

"Of course not. But, as a Mensa, it helped me to get funding, other research grants, so that I could do my research, and that took money."

"But you are working for Scion, correct? Getting paid? A company which you do not own?"

"Yes, absolutely," she said. "I'm working out of Paris for Scion Labs."

"Are you a shareholder?"

She glanced at Griffin and then slowly nodded. "Yes, I am."

"Did you have any issues with the board? Over your research?" Kerrick asked.

Before she had even answered Kerrick's question, Griffin asked, "Is that how you got to do the research that you were looking to do?"

"Well, I would hope the board had no issues with my

research, but it wouldn't surprise me if they had an issue *with me*," she said. "But I invested enough money in the company's shares that they couldn't argue about my research area, and I had a say in my own work."

"And do you think that may have pushed Hinkleman into doing what he did?"

She frowned. "I never considered what my shareholder entrance into the company might have done to him. But it's possible." She shrugged. "I own a fair bit of the company."

"A controlling interest?" Kerrick asked.

"Not half of the company, no," she said with a shake of her head.

"And what if Hinkleman suddenly found out that you were one of the major shareholders? Would that make him hate you?"

"He hates me anyway," she said. "He was all fire and brimstone when he was young, but none of his research panned out, so he's jealous of anybody who's on target and getting validated results."

"Which you think you are?"

"Which I definitely am," she said with a nod.

"Interesting," he said. "But it all comes back to that company, Scion Labs, and to Hinkleman."

"And potentially my ex. And potentially an enemy of my father too. Hinkleman said something about being paid from multiple sources. But I have no clue who that enemy of my father could be. Still, someone needs to warn him that he might have a viper close to home that he doesn't know about."

"Aah," Kerrick said, settling back. "That then makes sense of something that Brandon overheard. Makes a lot of sense now."

"What sense? Hinkleman just picks a victim, finds out how many people hate her and want her locked up, then he charges the people for kidnapping her?" she asked in outrage. "And how's that something to do with your life? Or …" She sat back. "Did someone approach Hinkleman?"

"The questions are then, who chose you, why did they choose you, and how is it that Hinkleman got involved?"

"He was the boss at the prison," she said, "so he's got to be involved with other patients as well."

"Is he a medical doctor?"

She looked at him in surprise. "I think he is. He was an MD first, and then I think he went into research because he didn't have the right kind of bedside manner for patient care relationships."

The two men stared at her, then slipped a covert glance to each other.

She wondered what that look was about but shrugged. "I just heard something about it."

"Between you and Brandon, you guys hear a lot, don't you?"

Brandon nodded, obviously listening but too busy eating still.

Amanda nodded toward him. "As Brandon said, he is a child. Nobody thinks he's important," she said. "In my case, I just put it down to being blonde and female. A lot of times men talk over us as if the conversation is just way too complicated for our fluffy empty brains."

"Well, you can bet we won't make that mistake," Kerrick said drily.

She looked at him with a smile and said, "You've already saved our lives. I don't even know how to begin to thank you."

"No thanks are necessary," he said. "But, if more people are being held there, like Brandon mentioned Cynthia and Peter, we wanted to make sure that we get everybody out. And …"

"Now that they know you two have escaped, the bad guys are already moving the rest of the prisoners," Griffin said. "I videoed as much as I could. While I was there, I saw three ambulances leave with six people total, two in each emergency vehicle."

Brandon perked up. "So that's why you left your face blacked out?"

Griffin laughed and nodded.

"Patients leaving in the same condition as they arrived?" Kerrick asked. "Meaning, likely all drugged into unconsciousness?"

"Yes," Griffin said. "You know that's the easiest way."

"They drugged us at night anyway," Amanda said in a low tone.

"But they've got to have a second location already set up and ready for the patients," Kerrick said, "particularly if they aren't ambulatory."

"Our guys are working on it," Griffin told Amanda. Then he picked up his cup of coffee and took a long sip.

As far as Amanda was concerned, Kerrick and Griffin were no ordinary team. Why did she think these rescue teams would entail at least eight guys? Or at least four to handle contingencies? But she admitted that Kerrick and Griffin were not any ordinary men either. They each counted as two men at least. Even so, but for the two of them, she hadn't seen anyone else helping out yet.

But that chat window was very interesting. She wasn't the super IT person that she wanted to be, but she knew enough about computers to hide her tracks when she moved around her research material. And that chat window of Kerrick's opened up into something very deep. She wouldn't be at all surprised if it wasn't some kind of black-ops or deep government covert operation link, superprivate, supershielded. She wanted to immediately get back into it and ask to get the information that she needed. Likely she'd get bumped out immediately.

"Well, surely somebody needs to pick up Hinkleman, while you search for others involved in kidnapping and that jail," she said, "because that's the one guy I can guarantee you was involved since I saw him in person at the jail."

"There's an alert out for him right now," Griffin said. "And on several other people involved, based on Brandon's descriptions and facial matches. We're on it. We just have to keep low until we know that everybody involved has been picked up."

"How long do we 'have to keep low'?" Her gaze went from one to the other. And back again.

They both shrugged and said, "A day? Maybe two."

She frowned and then realized she'd already spent a couple days as a prisoner, so how was a couple days being free, but with them, any different? She nodded. "Just make sure you get *all* these guys. I don't want to keep looking over my shoulder after this. And I surely don't want them after Brandon."

Brandon smiled a toothy grin her way, still chewing up the chicken in his mouth.

She patted his shoulder, then stood, looked at the beds, and asked, "How are we doing the sleeping arrangements?"

"The two beds here are for you and Brandon. One of us will sleep in the other room, while the other will be on watch here."

She nodded, walked to the bed closest to the window, and said, "In that case, I'm heading for some shut-eye."

Brandon decided he had enough food for now and said, "Me too," as he crawled into the bed across from her.

She smiled sleepily at him, forgetting to make him take a real shower before going to bed.

Then the two of them crashed and immediately fell asleep.

KERRICK RAISED HIS head from the pillow to find it was six o'clock in the morning, and he was about to switch shifts with Griffin. He heard a sound from the adjoining motel room. As Griffin's distinctive footsteps came his way, Kerrick hopped out of bed and walked into the bathroom. Quickly he used the facilities and scrubbed his face. Then he stepped out to see Griffin crawling into the other bed.

"All clear," Griffin whispered.

Kerrick nodded and headed to the desk. He took his laptop and his phone with him to the adjoining room. As he moved into Amanda and Brandon's room, Kerrick stopped to study the two sleeping people. He wasn't sure how this op had grown from saving one to two people from the get-go, but no way would he have dumped a child in the street on his own.

Although this one might be perfectly capable of handling himself, it was also obvious that he had a ton of information that was beneficial to their op; plus they needed to keep him close for his own safety. Brandon could potentially help find his dad as well as saving the other people held against their will by Hinkleman and his crew.

But what surprised Kerrick was to find both Amanda and Brandon curled up in the same bed, her arms wrapped around the child. Kerrick frowned, wondering what had happened.

Just then she opened her eyes, looked at him, smiled, and whispered, "Nightmares. No matter what kind of superbrain he has, he's still a child."

Kerrick nodded in understanding and walked over to their table, then set up his equipment. After that, he went back to the little kitchenette, where he plugged in the kettle and made himself an instant coffee. He would be up now until the day was over and needed something to keep him going.

When he passed by them, he saw Amanda slip out of bed and move into the bathroom. He expected her to go back to sleep after that, so he sat down at the table with a notepad, collating the notes they had. He was still waiting on more information and even updates. So far, nothing had come in. At least not via his phone. He hoped, when he hooked up to the internet, more information would be downloaded to his email and that the chat window sat there, waiting to help him. Preferably with answers.

He opened up his email program and waited. He heard beeps, notifying him as various emails dropped into his program. He quickly surveyed them, picked the couple that were the most important, and read some history on the background of Hinkleman, with a note that he was still at large. And then on Amanda's ex-husband. Thinking over things, he frowned, opened up the chat box, and typed,

**Have you picked up the ex-husband?**

**No.**

**Why?**

**No sign of him.**

**Crap.**

**Yes. We found the blue car in the bottom of the canal. And an older pickup.**

He grinned. **Good. Anyone in it?**

**You were right. Stanley and Tom were found dead inside, one in each. Jimmy has been picked up for questioning. We expect him to be arrested.**

**Good to know. Sounds like someone is cleaning up. Is her father safe? Did you inform him of her status and what she was told?**

**So far he's safe. And, yes, he was brought up-to-date.**

After that update, he added some reminders. **I don't have full research into the company that Hinkleman and Amanda were working for.**

**It's in your email.**

He returned to his email and looked. And there it was, hidden among all the rest. He brought it up and hunkered down to study the information. When Amanda came out of the bathroom, she walked over to the kitchenette and had a glass of water. She studied him, leaning against the counter.

He didn't even bother looking up. "It's still early. Just go back to bed."

"What about you?"

"I'm on shift watch now," he said. He flicked through the online pages, quickly scanning them. "I'm studying the company that you work for."

"If you find anything juicy, let me know," she said. She stifled a yawn, a movement that was both graceful and not, all at the same time. Kerrick found Amanda and Brandon to be fascinating with their massive brains, and yet, in some ways, both of them were so normal and even childlike in their innocence. She stumbled on her way back to bed, and he half stood, afraid she needed assistance, but she waved him off and said, "I'm just tired."

She made it to Brandon's bed, pulled back the covers gently so as to not disturb Brandon, slipped under them, softly laying her arm across Brandon's chest, and crashed.

There was just something so disarming about seeing her like this. So far, she'd escaped her cell, then went on to save Brandon, almost escaping the building itself when he and Griffin had found them. It took a lot of guts for her to do what she did. It took a lot of courage to go back after Brandon too. He wondered often about the maternal instincts in women and whether they were all blessed with equal amounts or whether some were just so much more caring.

No doubt she had formed an attachment to the young boy and he with her, and maybe that was a good thing. They were two of a kind. Nothing quite like bonding in captivity. They were good for each other. They both appeared to be loners, each with a father potentially distant, and maybe they needed each other. Amanda had been married but had no children, at least according to her file. He looked over to ask her but realized she was out cold. So he went back to reading his research.

About an hour later Kerrick heard a whimper. He looked over to see Brandon tossing fitfully in bed, crying out words. They were unintelligible, but he was still disturbed. Kerrick frowned, not sure how to help a child like this. He could tell him that it was okay, that he was caught up a nightmare, but Kerrick didn't want to wake him and scare him because that would be one of the worst things he could do. But, at the same time, how did you soothe a child like this?

As he watched, Amanda woke up, kicked off the covers, rolled over, slipping over to the far side, and cuddled up against Brandon. Kerrick could hear her voice as she rubbed the boy's shoulder and arm, whispering, "*Ssh*, it's okay, Brandon. We're safe now."

Almost immediately the child went quiet and went back to sleep.

Kerrick thought she was asleep too, but, as he continued to work on his laptop, she murmured, "What are you doing?"

"Making sure we get all the information we need," he said.

"Why don't you come lie down on my bed," she said. "I can't sleep while you're working."

He stopped and said, "I'm on duty."

"You need sleep too," she said.

"I'm fine."

"Well, I'm not," she said. "I can't sleep while you're doing that."

He frowned.

She rolled over, slipped out of Brandon's bed, crawled back onto her bed, and glared at him. "I'm not kidding."

"What the hell?" he muttered under his breath. Then he looked at her. "Surely you don't expect me to lie down and cuddle you, like you were doing with the child."

She sat up, looked at him, and said, "Expect? No, but would it help me get back to sleep, yes." And, with that, she flopped back down, pulled the covers over her shoulders, and stared at the wall.

He didn't know what to say. So, completely nonplussed,

he got up, slowly walked over, and laid down on top of the covers, wrapped an arm around her and tucked her back up against his warm body. It took about thirty seconds, and then she let go of a really heavy and deep sigh from inside her chest. He could almost feel it rattling up her spine as she slowly let it out, and he realized all that she had been through and how hard it must be to close her eyes with strangers hanging around. "I'm sorry," he murmured. "I didn't realize."

She gave a tiny shrug of her shoulders, the movement almost imperceptible. But tucked up so close as they were, he could feel it.

He whispered against her head and hair, "Just sleep. It'll all be better now." He watched her eyes flutter closed and her breathing drop into a heavy and steady rhythm. The little heart-shaped scar on her cheek caught his eye. He found himself leaning over to kiss the spot ever-so-gently. Surprised, he sagged back and held her close. That had come out of nowhere. Or maybe not, … not since he'd first seen that image of her.

Overwhelmed, he lay close to her, letting the emotions flow through him, marveling at the strength of them. He'd been so afraid such feelings were lost to him with the death of his wife. But Amanda was a special woman, and he'd instinctively recognized how special she was to him …

He waited several more moments, wondering how this woman could appear so strong and so caring, and yet, at the same time, so vulnerable. He found himself not wanting to leave her, not wanting her to face the boogeyman alone, who would surely come and catch her while she was asleep.

Nightmares were like that. They were insidious dream-stealing gremlins that came into your world when you couldn't protect yourself from them. They snuck into your subconscious and twisted everything into this nasty fog and then woke you up in a panic, fear sweating through your pores.

He gently stroked her arm, reaching around to lace her fingers with his. She shuffled slightly, moving back closer against him, spoon style, and he lay here knowing he needed to get up. But it was so comforting, even to him, to just lie here and hold her. And that was dangerous.

Knowing that he was crossing a line that he didn't dare cross, he slowly disengaged himself and pulled back a little bit to let the cool air slide up between them, so she could adjust to his leaving faster, before finally sitting up. At the edge of the bed, he stopped, looked down at her, and smiled because she hadn't moved. She was now in a deep sleep, and she needed it. Her body had to recover, and that would take longer than one night's sleep.

He sat down at the table to see a chat box had brought up more information. He quickly jumped back into his research, but he couldn't stop thinking about the warm and incredible woman he'd been holding for the last twenty minutes and how much he wanted to go back and hold her all over again.

# CHAPTER 10

W HEN AMANDA WOKE up later that same morning, she lay in bed, her mind still hazy and fuzzy. She had memories of warm arms wrapped around her, and it took her a moment to take stock and to realize she was alone in her bed. So, had that been a dream? She cast her mind back to earlier this morning, remembering the number of times she'd gone over to Brandon to soothe and ease the child back into sleep.

And her related conversation with Kerrick popped into her mind. She flushed, remembering how much she'd wanted him to come and lie beside her, wanting, like Brandon, to feel safe and secure, if only for a moment. And the fact that Kerrick had? … It had helped as she'd dropped into a deep sleep and even now felt one hundred times better. Her body and her mind would still take some time to recover, but she'd come a long way and all because of a good sleep. She slowly sat up and yawned. And looked over to see Griffin. She stretched and yawned again.

He smiled and said, "Good morning."

"Good morning," she said in a low voice, realizing from the light in the room that it was morning. "What time is it?"

"It's after nine," he said. "You slept well."

She stared at him in surprise and softly exclaimed, "I never sleep in."

"Well, there were extenuating circumstances this time," he said with a smile.

She nodded. "I'm glad to see Brandon is still sleeping."

"Absolutely. Kerrick's gone to shower and change," he said. "At ten o'clock we'll eat, whether Brandon's awake or not."

She chuckled at that. "It's guaranteed to wake him up if you bring food in here." She laid back down on the bed, content to just lie under the covers, feeling the softness under her back, knowing that her time in that nightmarish prison was over with. "Did you guys get any more answers?"

"Some but not too many. There's no sign of your ex or Hinkleman, but our people are watching for them. We've got the research on your company happening, and, according to the administrators, Hinkleman has taken a three-month leave of absence."

She snorted at that. "A sabbatical?"

"I don't know if you can call it that when it's from a company, at least one like this," he said. "But it's a leave of absence. That's all they would say."

"Well, *I* might be able to get them to say more, as a shareholder, but you probably have as much access as I do," she said, losing half the words in yet another yawn. She repeated her statement and then said, "But I need to be a little more awake for that."

"Well, I can offer you instant coffee or instant coffee," he said cheerfully.

She struggled with the concept and carefully said, "Caffeine is caffeine, and I can't afford to be choosy right now."

"True enough." He got up and put on the teakettle. "When I said it was nine, I really meant it was nine-twenty. So, it's almost nine-thirty now. Caffeine will help to get you awake and alert."

Amanda nodded, went into the bathroom, and washed her face. Her hair was a mess, having slept on it while wet. She hadn't even braided her shoulder-length locks. It was almost too short for a braid now, though, having cut it a few weeks before she had been taken prisoner. She ran her fingers through it, to loosen it up, and then took the brush to it. She smiled as she held the brush. The guys had a bag of toiletries for her, but none for Brandon. After all, they were only expecting to rescue her. By the time she brushed out the tangles in her hair, she felt a little bit better and a little more cognizant.

As she stepped out of her bathroom, Kerrick walked out of the bathroom in his adjoining motel room. Once all four of them were together in their rooms, the adjoining door had never been closed between them. He only had a towel wrapped around him as he sorted through clothes on the bed. She immediately averted her gaze but not before she saw the lean muscle, the sculpted abs, and that careful, and yet, very contained can-do determination on his face. She didn't want her first meeting with him to be awkward, but now it felt even more awkward.

She walked back to her bed, quickly made it up under Griffin's curious eyes, and then sat down at the table across from him. He nudged a cup of black liquid toward her. She stared at it and tried hard not to curl her lip.

"I know how you feel," he said, laughing. "But remember that *coffee is coffee* right now. When we get some food in you, we can get some of the real stuff too, but …"

She nodded and tugged the cup a little bit closer. When it was cool enough, she lifted it and took a small sip. Like he said, coffee was coffee, and she really had no right to complain after the sludge she'd been fed the last couple days in her prison cell. As she sank back into her chair, Kerrick joined them on this side and cast her a curious glance. He didn't appear worried by the previous event in the wee morning hours and didn't look bothered by the daytime recognition of having slept together, in the strictest sense, where she felt both, only for different reasons.

"You look better," he said.

She nodded. "I finally managed to get a deep sleep. Thanks." She tried to keep her tone neutral and noncommittal. If he could talk to her like they were friendly strangers, that worked for her too. It's not like they were any more than that. The fact that he was a stunning male and had held her so gently so she could go to sleep wasn't something she wanted to bring up with Griffin here. But she appreciated it nonetheless. She motioned toward Brandon. "He's still sound asleep."

"The innocence of a child," Kerrick said. "Oh, now we're back to instant coffee too?" He looked at Griffin, raising a brow.

"You can go," Griffin said. "The fresh air will help you out. I want to finish tidying up these notes first."

"What are we going for?" she asked.

"Coffee and breakfast," Griffin said without lifting his head.

"Do I get to choose what I want for breakfast?"

"As long as it comes from one of the two fast-food chains around the corner, yes," Kerrick said cheerfully.

She winced. "I need a lot of food though. I'm really hungry."

"I doubt it's anything compared to what Brandon will need," Kerrick said. "I'd ask if you wanted to come with me, but I don't want you outside. We need to keep you hidden. We can't take the chance that somebody is tracking you."

"Could they find me if I was just walking around the corner?"

"It's an intersection," Griffin interrupted. "And that could quite easily mean cameras. And we use the street cameras ourselves for facial recognition to track anybody we can, so I suspect they will too."

"Do we really think it's that high class for Hinkleman and his crew?"

"No," Kerrick said. "I doubt *high class* has anything to do with it. But a lot of money and time went into outfitting that prison and keeping you all fed. There were pallets and pallets of food in the loading docks, so chances are quite a few people are involved. And it wouldn't take much to have security cams and traffic cameras searched. I've already done it myself to find the vehicle you were kidnapped in. That's ultimately how I found you at the sanitorium."

She looked at him in surprise. "We never did go over those details, did we?"

He gave her a half smile, paired with warm eyes. "You were a little tired."

"And weak, true," she said. "But that's hardly an excuse."

He cocked his head curiously. "You don't let yourself off the hook much, do you?"

"I feel like I'm always playing catch-up," she said, then smiled and nodded. "Well, I would much prefer to come along for the walk to get the food. But if you think it's that dangerous …"

"We can't take the chance right now," Griffin said, his tone a little brisker. "Kerrick, if you want to go now, we'll try to rouse Brandon. In the meantime …"

Kerrick laughed and took the hint. He was out the door within seconds.

Amanda glanced at Griffin. "Is it safe for him to go alone?"

"It's not safe to leave you guys alone," Griffin answered quietly. "So, we stay together as much as possible, but one of us will always have to leave to run various errands."

She nodded and sipped her coffee again. "I don't even know anything about the two of you or how you came together or who sent you after us."

"Unfortunately I have yet to find anybody who's reported Brandon missing, not even his dad, Mr. Coleman," he whispered, changing the topic. "I'm not sure how long Brandon was there either."

Her gaze dropped to the sleeping boy, and she shook her head, whispering, "I only met him yesterday. He tapped Morse code on the floor of his cell, which was the ceiling of my cell, and I answered."

"And how many people in the world," Griffin said with a headshake, "could communicate via Morse code?"

"Well, thankfully he tried," she said. "Otherwise, I wouldn't have known he was there."

"How many doors did you try on his floor?"

"All of them," she said immediately. "Also I tried every door I came to on my floor, but they were all locked except for one, a broom closet. Then I went up one floor, did the same, and found another closet where several coveralls were stored plus some keys, including *the* master key."

He leaned forward and asked, "You serious?"

She got up and felt her pockets. Down at the bottom, she pulled out the key and held it up. "That's how I got into

Brandon's cell."

He looked at it and whistled.

"We need to go back and see if anybody's left in that place," Amanda said, sitting down hard and staring at him. "And we've wasted the rest of the night and this morning sleeping instead of helping them."

"No need. Another group, like me and Kerrick, was there, keeping watch."

"Well, they shouldn't have let the kidnappers leave with those victims. The other team should have gone in and found as many of the victims as they could."

"They're also tracking where the kidnappers are taking their victims now. And I know that's hard to hear, but this is more than just finding those kidnapped people. We have to go to the evil beginning of all this."

She sagged into place, staring at him, and then shook her head. "Not if still more people are there."

"If they haven't already done that third check of the facility, I can get this key to somebody who will send in a team, and they'll check every room."

"I feel so terrible," she whispered. "I should have remembered this last night."

"Hey, this key is not the end of the world. Most of the guys in my world can get into those doors without a key. I know that a search was done, so let's hold off until I can get more information."

She nodded, but inside she felt sick to her stomach. "For those people to stay even one more night, it's too much."

"And the kidnappers are being followed and tracked too, but we also can't afford to get involved in heavy gunfire where some of these patients might get hurt as collateral damage. You also have to consider that maybe they'll kill some of these people in order to stop them from talking."

"According to Brandon, they were all unconscious."

"Which begs the question, why weren't you and him?"

She frowned at him, but her mind was agile. "I was knocked out originally."

"So maybe they didn't need to drug you because you already couldn't fight back."

"Or because Hinkleman needed me lucid, at least at certain times."

Just then Griffin's phone went off with a weird buzzing sound. He lifted it, looked down, and smiled. "Kerrick's ordering."

"Can he carry it all back?"

Griffin nodded. "But it'll be a lot just because of Brandon's appetite."

"Fine," she said, "but I'd rather have news about that prison."

He typed away on his laptop, and she stared at him suspiciously, wondering if he had access to information that he wasn't sharing. But, of course, he did. She didn't even know what group he was affiliated with. "What country do you work for?"

He lifted his head, stared at her, and smiled. "And why would you assume that I'm from another country?"

"Because of your accent," she said.

"And what accent do I have?"

"American," she said decisively. "Is this a US-government operation?"

"Well, if it is, it sure had better be with the agreement of England's MI6 and MI5 divisions."

She sank back on her chair. "Good luck with that. Everybody does the secret spy stuff. I wonder how much any country knows what goes on in another country, much less in their own backyard."

"Just as a courtesy," he said, "we always operate by letting people know where and what we're up to."

"Sure you do," she said with a knowing smile. "But that doesn't mean that they've acknowledged it or allowed it, have they?"

"We are here with the full agreement of your French government, the UK government, even Norway's government."

She wondered about that. "So my father's behind this? Didn't somebody say that he contacted you?" Griffin was silent on that, but she nodded. "Kerrick said something about that. He told me that my father put out the call."

"Are you close to him?"

Her smile flashed. "Yes, we're very close."

"How close?"

She sipped her coffee several more times and studied him over in the rim of the cup. "I'm not sure what you're asking."

"Would he have had a hand in keeping you as a prisoner?"

She shook her head in an instant. "No, of course not."

Griffin didn't say anything. He just continued to watch her steadily.

She could feel the flush walking up her cheeks, but she remained adamant. "No, he would *not* have been behind this. I'm surprised he still doesn't have one of his security details following me around all the time, like he did during my college days. Because of his wealth and his life in politics, he's become very defensive." She stopped, inhaled a gasp, and stared. "He still has a security detail on me, doesn't he?"

Her gaze widened. "That's how he knew I was missing, isn't it?"

Griffin's eyebrows shot up. "That's something we can check."

"We need to and then find out how they lost me. I believe Hinkleman said," she recalled, as the memory flooded back in, "that somebody was trying to punish my father, I think. Or maybe it was blackmail." She rubbed at her temples. "Sorry, the details are really fuzzy. I don't know what damn drugs they gave me, but I'd wake up in the morning to realize that people had been in my cell while I was out cold. It's a very disconcerting feeling."

"How did you know?"

"The chamber pot had been emptied," she said with a grimace. "I was really surprised at that, but they were full, so what can you do?"

"Well, if they wanted to keep you healthy, then they had to keep you disease-free. And that means emptying chamber pots," he said with a nod. "The drug was probably just something to help you sleep deeper, so that they could come in and do what they needed to do without you waking up."

"Maybe," she said, "but it's an awful feeling to wake up and to know that somebody has been there, looking at you while you sleep."

"That stage of your life is over now. I'm surprised you slept as well as you did."

She flushed but didn't say anything. A voice from one of the beds saved her from that moment as Brandon called out, "Hello?"

What a painful and lonely cry, as if Brandon were still at the prison. Amanda immediately stood, headed to the bed, and said, "Hey, glad you're awake."

He rubbed his eyes and sat up. "We really are safe, right?"

She nodded. "We really are, yes."

He opened his arms, and she reached down, sitting on the edge of the bed, and hugged him.

"Thank you for helping me sleep in the night," he said. "I kept waking up, thinking somebody bad was there, but it was always you."

"Hey," she said, "not an issue. I'm just happy that you're doing okay. It was a pretty long night."

"Yeah," he said. He yawned and then rubbed his face back and forth against her shoulder. "And I'm still tired."

"That's because it's been a rough couple days. Do you know how long you've been in that prison?"

"Nine nights."

Amanda glanced at Griffin. He stared at Brandon in surprise. "So," Griffin said, "you didn't come in at the same time as Amanda?"

Amanda shook her head. "I was only there a few nights, I think. I honestly can't tell you that because I don't know how long I might have been drugged. For all I know, I was brought in the same time as these other people, and what I thought was my first day when I finally woke up could have been my second or third day there." She frowned at that, not liking the idea at all. "What day is it?"

Griffin smiled. "Tuesday. The Tuesday after your kidnapping on the previous Sunday. So you were with the kidnappers about thirty-six hours."

"Seemed longer," Amanda said, turning to Brandon. "I'm so sorry you were there for so long." She hugged him again. "The darkness distorted all my senses. Not to mention the drugs. So my stay felt interminable."

Griffin said, "Let's get you a little more awake, Brandon. Kerrick is coming back with food any moment now."

At that, Brandon hopped out of bed and ran to the bathroom. While he was gone, Amanda quickly made up his bed, picked up the clothes he had dumped on the side, walked over to the bathroom, and knocked. He opened the door, and she handed him his shorts, T-shirt, and socks. "Get fully dressed so that we can be ready to move if needed."

His face was serious as he nodded, and she loved the fact that he understood. As she returned to join Griffin, he smiled. "You'll enjoy being a mother."

"Well, that's an interesting issue because who knows if I'll ever be a mom? It's not like I've had much practice at it."

"No other siblings?" he asked.

She shook her head. "No, none. Although I was married for six months, I never got pregnant during that time. Which turned out to be a good thing."

When Brandon came out fully dressed, his face was washed, and the hair around the edges of his face was damp from his ablutions. She chuckled and motioned at the table. Kerrick was just coming up the stairs outside, and Griffin was already clearing off his work from the table.

"Go sit down," Griffin told Brandon. "Food's coming."

Brandon raced to the edge of the table and sat, looking at the front door.

As soon as the door opened, and Kerrick stepped in, Brandon gave him a huge cheerful wave and said, "Good timing. I'm starved."

KERRICK CHUCKLED AS he unloaded the multiple bags he

carried. "Needed two people to haul this load," he complained good-naturedly.

"Well, I offered to go with you," Amanda said as she opened the first bag and took out a selection of items. "What did you get?"

"Four stacks of pancakes," he said. "Hash browns, patties, scrambled eggs, sausages, breakfast sandwiches." Then he shrugged. "I bought as much as I could reasonably carry in one load."

She looked at him in astonishment. "Were you expecting us to eat it all?"

"I highly suspect that, what we as a group can't eat, Brandon will finish off later," he said. "Particularly if he's anything like I was at his age."

"Did you order the same for everybody?"

He nodded. "Check the other bags for more food. I ordered four of everything."

Beside her, Brandon cried out a yes as he was handed a stack of pancakes. And then Amanda upended a massive baggie of small individual servings of syrup and butter. Brandon dug in without waiting for anybody else. Kerrick sat down, looked at Griffin, and asked, "Any changes or any updates?"

"No, nothing yet from our assistants. But Brandon says he was there for nine days, and Amanda found a master key to the prison rooms," he said, holding it up from where he had it on the table. Kerrick looked from the key to Amanda and raised an eyebrow. She quickly explained.

He nodded and said, "Good thinking and lucky that you found it."

"At that time, I have to admit I didn't question it. But now I'm wondering if it wasn't a setup."

"Possibly," he said. "But nobody came after us, so, if it was, and they expected to catch you, it doesn't really matter now because you're free."

"But I want to make sure that nobody else was left behind and that some operation is overseeing the kidnappers taking off with their victims."

"There was an operation in motion, yes. We'll be told when we're told."

He could see she didn't like that answer though. He seemed to be on a need-to-know basis as it was. If he asked the right question, he would get answers, but it was hard to imagine all the questions that he needed to ask. He wished his new boss was more forthcoming.

He bit into a big breakfast sandwich with sausage patties and eggs, as Brandon beside him dove into the pancakes. Kerrick loved to see the kid eat, especially since he had apparently gone without meals for a long time. Even one meal a day for nine days wasn't enough for any growing child. The food on their table disappeared at a rate that Kerrick expected, but the look on Amanda's face was surprise at Brandon's appetite. Finally Kerrick reached out a hand and said to Brandon in a low voice, "It's okay. There'll be more food."

He could see Brandon almost stopping, as if really understanding what Kerrick said, then the boy nodded slowly. "Meaning, I don't have to eat it all right now, correct?"

"Exactly."

Brandon nodded, put down his fork, and settled back. "Then I think I'm full."

"Good," Amanda said. "There will be some leftovers. Not too many though."

"And we can get more food if we need to," Griffin added

with a wink to Brandon.

Brandon was all smiles.

"I'll drop this in the garbage bin outside." Kerrick rose and cleaned up the empty dishes and packaging. Not very much was left at all. One breakfast sandwich, a couple sausage patties, and a few hash browns. He put everything together in one of the containers and set it atop the table and then left the room and tossed their garbage into a big trash bin in the back of the motel. After that, he took a quick pass around the perimeter of the motel to make sure everything was clear.

Ever since he'd left this morning to go to the restaurant, he'd had that feeling of being followed. A sense of something not quite right. As he came around to the parking lot again, he saw a large suburban against the fence on the far side of the front parking area. It had smoked-out windows and looked government-issued. And that was disturbing because, as far as Kerrick understood, *he* was government, and his UK counterpart was to keep him in the loop.

Slipping around back, taking the external staircase to the second floor, he made half a lap around the building on the walkway that led to all the motel room doors. Now at the front of the motel, yet on the far corner from the suspect vehicle, he would be exposed on these exterior stairs and landings. So he crouched below the railing level and crept all the way across to the far side. Around this corner should be the SUV. He stood up and carefully peered around the edge to see if the vehicle was still there. It was. At least he knew where the interlopers were, but, not liking anything about this, Kerrick sent a text to Griffin.

Griffin stood, opened the door, and didn't show his face. Kerrick dashed inside and looked at him. "This can't be good," he said.

Then the chat window pinged, followed by the ring of a weird little bell.

Griffin looked at the laptop screen and said, "*Move now.*"

The two men galvanized into action. While Amanda collected their few belongings, Kerrick raced to the back of the motel room and looked out the window at the fire escape. He opened up the window enough so that they could scramble out, but it would take precious minutes to get everybody outside. He quickly ordered Amanda out the window and got her into the fire escape with his help. Instead of going down, they went up to the rooftop, Kerrick explaining to her that Griffin had Brandon in his care. Then, from his rooftop perch, Kerrick chose another fire escape for them to take all the way down.

Meanwhile, Griffin brought up the last of the equipment, and he tossed Brandon on his back, and said, "Hang on." He quickly landed in the fire escape, and, with Brandon still holding tight, Griffin raced up the fire escape, onto the rooftop, and then to the far side, taking another fire escape, meeting Kerrick and Amanda at the bottom. Griffin handed off the equipment, transferred Brandon to Kerrick's back, and said, "I'll be back in two." He disappeared around the left of the motel.

With Amanda looking on with terror on her face, Kerrick knew Brandon was in the same fearful state because of the grip he had around his neck. He smiled at her reassuringly. "Griffin's gone to get his wheels."

She nodded slowly. "But won't they know it's him?"

"Maybe," he said. "If they follow us, we will lose them again. It's what we do."

Just then a vehicle came around and headed right for them. Amanda, crying out a muffled surprise, dashed to the side. Kerrick reached out and caught her, then held her close and said, "It's Griffin."

"But it's not our car."

Griffin heard her. He opened the window and gave her a grim smile. "Ours had a tracker on it. Whether that's factory original or a very new addition, not good for our purposes."

With them stashed in the back seat, Kerrick quickly ran to the far side and hopped into the passenger's seat as Griffin took off. Kerrick brought up his laptop, ready to access the chat box and get some safe house info. When they pulled out of the parking lot on the far side, he glanced behind to see if they were being followed. But, so far, he saw no sign of anybody. "Well," he said, "I wish I knew who that vehicle belonged to."

"Check their license plate number," Griffin said, tossing him his phone. "I took a photo of it."

Kerrick quickly grabbed the phone, typed in the license plate info into his laptop, and did a check. "It's not coming up."

"Interesting," Griffin said.

Kerrick typed it into the chat window and asked for clarification.

The answer came back. **British Secret Intelligence Service.**

**Legit?**

**Yes. But driver isn't. Vehicle was stolen in the last forty-eight hours.**

He swore softly.

**BTW, Jimmy was found dead in his jail cell just an hour ago.**

**No surprise there. We're on the move.**

**We have a safe house.**

The address was typed into the bottom. He quickly brought it up on the GPS so that Griffin could follow the computer directions to get where they were going. Then he settled back to keep his eyes peeled on the roads around him. He didn't know what had just happened, how they had been found, but any change at this point wasn't good. Into the chat window, he asked for an update. Just then his phone rang. It was ID'd as Unknown Caller, and he answered it to hear the same tumblers clicking in his ear. After giving the preauthorized code word, a computerized voice came on, which sounded suspiciously like his friend Beta from the pub.

"The kidnappers' initial location was searched at five o'clock this morning," the computer said. "It's completely empty. No patients were left behind. It appears that only about ten rooms were in use, based on the garbage left behind. We have tracked three of the ambulances to two different locations. We're getting ready to do a sweep on those locations now."

Kerrick asked, "What about the other patients on Brandon's list?"

"No confirmation yet," he said. "But, from the time when you arrived there, we have had eyes on the place. Potentially they were taken out before."

"I can ask Brandon. He might have more to add."

"Maybe, but don't trust him too much. Also we don't know if either Brandon or Amanda has been inserted with a subcutaneous tracking device. They need to be fully checked out."

"Where will that happen?"

"At the safe house."

And then his phone went dead. The thought of a tracking device didn't thrill him. But it would have been an easy thing to do when they were unconscious, particularly with the child. It would also explain why they'd been allowed to escape because they could easily track Amanda and Brandon and find out who was helping them. He looked at Griffin and said, "Tracking devices, the injected kind."

Griffin shot him a surprised look, contemplated it for a moment, and then nodded. "I presume a physical is in order?"

"Yes. At the safe house." Kerrick settled back for the drive ahead.

# CHAPTER 11

"TRACKING? WHAT THE hell does that mean?" Amanda had watched her fair share of spy movies, but this sounded like a script gone bad. She glanced at Brandon, who was calmer and more relaxed this time. He stared out the car window, almost inhaling the information as it flew by. But a tracking device could have been injected into either of them. She understood what a safe house meant in theory, but anything that was different and unique right now didn't make her feel any more confident. Sure, the men had taken them away from the motel when a threat had surfaced, and they'd had some good quality sleep there and had been fed, multiple times and in unending quantities. Now they were on the move but to where?

As she sat back, Brandon slipped his fingers into hers. She squeezed his hand gently and just held his. She, as an adult, had to give at least the outward appearance of being confident. To her, however, just the unknown element and the newness of this experience made for a rather terrifying experience. She lived in her lab, especially since her divorce. She rarely went out. She rarely dated. Everything that had happened in the last few days was well out of her comfort zone.

As were her out-of-the-blue maternal instincts. She'd never put much thought into having a family of her own after her divorce, choosing to bury herself in her work, but, after connecting with Brandon, how could she not want a son? Especially if he turned out anything like Brandon.

But, in order to see that future, she had to deal with her current mess. Hinkleman was one of the bigger and more urgent mysteries to solve here. What purpose did kidnapping her do for him? He still had all her research regardless. Could promote it as his alone.

Okay, yeah, joining forces with two other idiots who wanted her out of the way had lined his pockets with money. Money to do even more research. But wasn't that what Scion Labs was doing for him already? He was the chairman after all. A position that held a lot of prestige and power. How he got that position was a mystery for another day.

She couldn't find the logic in any of this because the bad guys weren't using logic as their metric. Theirs were more about money, power, greed. Again she shook her head.

Brandon squeezed her hand.

*Very intuitive kid.* She smiled down at him, squeezed his hand back, fighting another wave of anger at Mr. Coleman, Brandon's father. His actions were unthinkable. Kidnapping any child and mistreating him this way was evil, but allowing his own child to suffer through this? That was evil on a massive level. What she wouldn't do to get this sorry excuse for a father in a torture chamber and let her own rage take over.

But a tiny voice reminded her that she didn't have all the information. Yet.

And these thoughts brought her to her own failed marriage, which made no more sense than Hinkleman or Mr. Coleman. She had been so unimpressed with the state of her marriage that she'd promptly dumped her cheating spouse.

And fast. No man since had made her want to change her mind about the hallowed but flawed institution of marriage—until Kerrick.

Even with his ethics and honor and transparent communication evident for all to see, she wasn't sure what she was feeling. Just … something. Heat. Curiosity. Gratitude … and damn more heat. Now here she was—on the run, out of a job, her most precious research in the hands of a greedy madman—wishing for some kind of true real-life romance. *Stupid timing.*

Frowning, she remembered Kerrick mentioning that her ex-husband was off-grid. She leaned forward and said, "My ex has a cabin in Wales. If he's missing, he could very well be there. It's part of his original family homestead."

"Do you have an address?"

She frowned and shook her head. "No. I just remember him having grown up there and saying that he went back every year."

Kerrick nodded and said, "Let me pass that along." He pulled out his phone and sent some texts. "Do you know anything about his family?" he asked.

"Nothing that you can trust," she said simply. "As I found out too late, he was a consummate liar. He did tell me that he *supposedly* had an older brother and that his parents were *supposedly* dead and that his brother and he used to meet up at the cabin every once in a while. I guess I believe that last part most of all. Take it all for what it's worth, coming from a very unreliable narrator."

"So, you don't know if he has a brother or if his parents are dead is what you're saying?"

"Exactly. But I do think the cabin was for real because he talked about learning to fish there. And he always spoke with so much emotion tied to those memories."

"That's often a good indicator," Griffin said. He pulled to an intersection, put on his blinker, and turned left. "We are only a couple blocks away from our destination."

"Good," she said, "but is it any safer than our last one?"

"We'll have to see," he said. "I've never been to this one."

And that didn't inspire confidence either. She stiffened as they came around to what looked like a common residential area and pulled into a home with a double garage door that opened automatically as they approached.

"And that's not suspicious," she murmured.

"Just means we're expected," Kerrick said cheerfully.

"Sure, but do we know by whom?" she asked.

"We'll find out," he said, sending a quick text. "Remember. We're here to have your backs."

At that, Brandon piped up and said, "It's a safe house, so it's government-run, by one faction or the other. What we don't know at this point in time is which country. The governments like to keep it that way."

"Maybe so but don't you guys know which government?" Amanda asked Kerrick, then looked to Griffin.

"Good question," Griffin said.

"Wish we knew the answer," Kerrick added. Then his phone beeped, and he read the screen, smiling.

Amanda caught sight of that exchange and felt slightly more at ease. She turned to Brandon, hoping to distract him from the reality of his life right now. "I guess you're a big fan of spy movies too, huh?"

He grinned and said, "Absolutely. Especially the *Bond, James Bond* series."

"I like all those too," she murmured with a chuckle,

amused at Brandon's attempt to sound like Sean Connery, and also very surprised someone his age was familiar with the actor who first played James Bond.

Griffin shut off the engine and, after a quick and silent exchange of hand signals, both men hopped out. She was much slower to get out, and Brandon slid over to her side and exited the vehicle with her. As soon as they were inside, the garage door came down, and they walked into the main part of the house.

She froze. Two men and a nurse stood in front of them. The men nodded, acknowledging the presence of Kerrick and Griffin, but their eyes were on Amanda and Brandon.

One of the men was obviously the brawn, but the guy in the lab coat seemed to be the leader and spoke up. "We'll run some scans to make sure that you haven't been injected with anything. Particularly to confirm you're not carrying a tracking device."

"What kind of scans? Will they be invasive?" she asked, stepping closer to Brandon. Instinctively Brandon reached up and put his hand in hers.

"Just the swipe of a handheld wand for basic metal detection, like used in some American schools, and another one that's pretty high-tech to see if there are any foreign bodies within you, not just those minute metal invaders overlooked by the wand but those made of plastics or whatever."

"And what's the nurse for?" she asked, not moving from her spot. Griffin and Kerrick had aligned themselves on either side of the two of them, still protecting them. That did help a lot, but still she and Brandon were now in somebody else's stronghold and under somebody else's rules, and she didn't think much of that at all.

The nurse stepped forward and swept a handheld wand

over both her and the boy. "Clear," she announced to all in the room. "No large metal foreign objects found."

The lead man smiled at Amanda and said, "Just lie down on the bed. We're not doing any major surgery."

After a glance at both Griffin and Kerrick—who nodded gently to her—she walked slowly toward the man. He motioned for her to enter the next room, and she stepped forward hesitantly. There she saw some kind of a portable X-ray machine. Different but the same. She frowned. "Is this the only way?"

"It's the best way, the least invasive way," he said. Then he reached out a hand and introduced himself. "I'm Dr. Claussen."

Because he seemed to be a medical doctor, as evidenced by his white lab coat, her brows immediately came together in a frown. "If no major surgery will be done here today, are you expecting *some* level of your medical services to be needed?"

"I hope not," he said quietly. "But, if you do have a tracking device, it's likely subcutaneous, and somebody will need to remove it."

"I haven't noticed any recent injury," she said, slowly realizing she had had no way to adequately check any part of her back. She'd had had more pressing health issues to address, both of the physical and mental kinds, like surviving, like escaping, like dealing with poor Brandon's nightmares.

"Good," the doctor said. "Maybe you should go first. That'll make Brandon feel a little better about the process."

"Do I get to watch?" Brandon asked, in serious mode now. Obviously he wanted firsthand information on this.

Amanda spoke up. "I vote yes," her stare locking in on

Kerrick first, then Griffin.

"I don't think that is a good idea," stated Dr. Claussen.

"This boy has a higher IQ than me—and probably you," Amanda responded to Dr. Claussen, slightly amazed at the heat in her words. "If it's such a good idea for me to go first to convince Brandon how safe this procedure is, then Brandon should be an eyewitness of that before he decides whether to do this himself." In the lull that followed, Amanda added, "And he does get to decide himself. Right?" Again she stared at Kerrick and Griffin.

Kerrick grinned, sharing a knowing glance with Griffin, before speaking to the doc. "Mama Bear has spoken."

"Let me just state for the record," Dr. Claussen began with a huff, "that I do not agree to any of this."

Kerrick pulled out his special disposable phone. "No problem. We'll arrange for another doctor." He was already texting when Dr. Claussen cleared his throat.

The nurse with him nodded her head, giving him a pat on his arm.

"That won't be necessary. While highly irregular and not our standard methodology in my field, I realize these are trying times for the two of you and that your emotional health is as important as your physical health." Dr. Claussen faced Brandon. "I'll leave your medical decision up to you, young man."

Brandon was all smiles, and yet, surprised as he looked into the faces of all who surrounded him. "Cool!"

His simple happy reaction was a very welcome respite from the rest of this. And then reality brought Amanda back to the present. … Hating to go first, but smiling for Brandon's sake, Amanda shot a nervous glance at Kerrick, but he again nodded at her reassuringly. Following the doctor's instructions, she laid down on the temporary hospital bed that they had set up.

She noted the brawny stranger was camped out near the front windows of the safe house and felt a bit reassured.

"I want Brandon behind a lead shield," she said as he held her hand and stood beside the bed. "But … you two aren't wearing lead vests. Is there any chance of radiation exposure for Brandon?"

Dr. Claussen shook his head. "Not with this machine. It uses lasers instead."

Amanda felt somewhat better and smiled down at Brandon, whose entire focus was on the machinery in the room.

With the doctor's click of a handheld toggle switch, a series of X-rays were taken while the others remained standing nearby in the other room, with a direct view of the procedures.

She frowned, not that she had really stopped frowning since leaving the motel, and asked, "Won't it take a while to develop them?"

The nurse smiled. "No, not for this kind of X-ray. We'll have results very quickly."

"And, if I don't have a tracker, we still have to X-ray Brandon?"

The nurse nodded. "It's best if we do, yes."

Dr. Claussen asked Brandon if he could be X-rayed as well.

"Sure." Brandon was already climbing up on the hospital bed as Amanda stood up.

"Why don't you sit in the chair in the other room, Amanda, while we await your results?"

She was already shaking her head when Brandon piped up. "No. Why can't she stay here with me?"

The doctor gave in easily and quickly completed Brandon's scan. When done, the doctor said, "We expect your results, Amanda, in just a couple minutes."

"Literally?" she asked.

Dr. Claussen chuckled. And the nurse was already pulling something from the strange X-ray machine, like copies from a photocopier.

Over the instant objections of Dr. Claussen, both Kerrick and Griffin joined them in the makeshift hospital room, ready to see the official results.

With a resigned sigh, the doctor walked over and held the odd sheet in his hand. He held it up for her and the others to see. He pointed to the picture, at the base of the back of her neck, where something metallic was identified. It appeared on the picture as just a small dot.

Her hand immediately went to her hairline at the nape of her neck, and she felt a little bit of a scab but thought it was just a scratch from her rough treatment in the initial kidnapping event, not to mention Dr. Hinkleman's slap.

Dr. Claussen leaned forward to take a closer look at her neck, while the others gathered around the end of bed to stare at the photo laying there. "There are no stitches," he said. "It's simply been injected. The body is amazing in the sense that it will cover any injuries, no matter how slight, with scar tissue very quickly."

"So how do you get it out?" she asked, while seeing a picture of her head on the hospital bed and surrounded by everyone except their guard.

"I'll have to cut it out," he said quietly.

She stiffened, but Kerrick grabbed her shoulder and squeezed. "It'll be fine."

"So you say," she muttered, turning her head his way.

"It's not your head they're cutting into." And honestly, she didn't even realize they would do it right now until she felt the doctor's hand on her head, telling her to remain still. Then she felt a tiny cut slicing her skin, followed by a probe inserted briefly, before the doctor pulled out something so small she almost missed it. She studied the edge of his tweezers and saw a small metal ball, which could have been the end of the tweezers for all she knew. She looked up at him and said, "That's it?"

"Yes, that's that," he said. He put it carefully into a little test tube for safekeeping, slipping a metal casing over it. "This metal sleeve stops the tracking unit from sending out any signals."

The nurse now came over with Brandon's X-rays.

After a quick look, the doctor pulled out a second tube and turned to Brandon. "May I do a quick check of your neck, young man?"

"Sure." Brandon seemed to be in total research mode, happily taking in this new experience as both fieldwork and lab work. "Do I have the same thing in my head as Amanda?"

"Looks like it," the doctor said amiably. "Same place too."

Amanda gripped Brandon's hands and said, "It'll be over before you know it, and I hardly even felt it."

Brandon nodded, trying to be brave, but it was obvious that doctors and needles and surgical knives were a bit of an issue. She hugged him tightly. "I'll stay right here, holding you. Just focus on my face. Okay?"

Brandon's neck was exposed for the doctor to work with. He bent closer, took a quick look at the back of the child's neck. "It looks the same, like the scabbed-over scratch that I saw on the back on your neck, Amanda."

She and Brandon exchanged a look and then a nod. She squeezed his fingers when the doctor held Brandon's head still and made a tiny slice and popped out the same type of microdot that had been in her. He washed the wound carefully and then told Brandon that he was all done.

She frowned, asking the doctor, "Did you wash my incision?"

He chuckled. "Yes, I did."

"I didn't even realize it."

Brandon sat up and instinctively raised his hand to the wound, but she stopped him and said, "Let it heal for a few minutes, so you don't transfer any dirt or germs from your fingers and put it on the open cut."

He nodded and then immediately turned and asked the doctor, "May I see it?"

And there was that same bright and inquisitive child back again, jumping down from the hospital bed to stand closer to his tracking dot. *The miracle of youth.*

The doctor chuckled and held up the tube that contained his microdot, then placed a metal sleeve over it too.

"So what's on those dots?" Amanda asked.

"We assume tracking information," the doctor said, "but, until we get it analyzed, we don't know."

"So is it likely to have things like our medical records or what they did to us while imprisoned or just something to keep track of where we've been moved to?" She wrapped one arm around Brandon's shoulders and held him close.

"We expect just tracking info, but I don't know for sure yet."

On that note, she jerked, turned to look at Kerrick, and said, "That means they tracked us here. We can't stay now."

He nodded. "We never intended to. This is just a temporary stop to make sure that we don't get followed beyond this point."

"Were we followed?" she asked. "Are these people in danger too?" She pointed to the doc and his nurse, frowning again.

"Not followed that we noticed, no, but that doesn't mean the kidnappers aren't keeping track of us on a computer somewhere and, therefore, could come attack this place to reclaim its victims."

She looked back at the doctor. "So, you'll set up something here? To capture the kidnappers, or the people they'll send here, expecting to attack us?"

"That's a good idea," Dr. Claussen said, with a hand extended toward Kerrick and Griffin. "I don't handle that type of thing, but I'm sure the people in the know will have it all organized."

"It's already being set up," Kerrick said, a smile on his face.

"But we need to be long gone," Brandon piped up. "So where are we going next?"

Now that the ordeal with the surgeon's knife was over, Brandon seemed to be right in the midst of the action. And loving it.

She smiled down at him and said, "You're a brave little guy, aren't you?"

He grinned up at her. "Hey, we're in a spy movie. This is awesome."

She laughed, looked at Kerrick, and said, "Well, you appear to be our intrepid leader. Where to next?"

His phone beeped. He pulled it out and checked the screen. "I have the new address for us, so I suggest we fall back into the vehicle and head off again."

"How long to the next stop?" Brandon asked.

He shrugged. "Maybe fifty-five minutes."

"Good," Brandon said. "We need to stop somewhere on the way to pick up lunch."

Kerrick looked at him and raised an eyebrow. "There's still leftover breakfast."

"No, there isn't," he said. "I ate that already. And, besides, it's almost lunchtime." He rubbed his hands together with glee and raced toward the garage.

KERRICK DROVE CAREFULLY and steadily. He wondered how long before Amanda and Brandon noticed, considering they were both incredible geniuses. He wasn't sure if they were that practically minded when so blessed intellectually. But shortly thereafter Amanda leaned forward from the back seat and whispered, "Where are we going?"

He caught her gaze in the rearview mirror of the car. "You'll find out soon."

She gave him a quick frown but settled again in her seat. Brandon leaned against her as soon as she resettled. The farther away from the safe house they traveled, the clingier Brandon got. But she understood. She didn't know what would happen to him. His father hadn't reported him missing. Did he even know that Brandon was gone? How could he not be aware? What parent could be that clueless?

Unless Brandon was enrolled in some private school, but even school officials take note of student attendances—or absences. Or had Mr. Coleman, Brandon's own father, had a hand in this atrocity? That thought really bothered her.

Already she was game to adopt the boy. Legally.

Or whatever it took.

AS HE DROVE, Griffin talked on his phone incessantly in the passenger front seat, continually distracting Kerrick because the bits and pieces he heard were disturbing, to say the least. Brandon's father still couldn't be located, which, in Kerrick's opinion, could work out for the best for his kid and for people in general. Neither could their associates locate Hinkleman or Amanda's ex but not for lack of trying.

Kerrick was afraid that, every step of the way, people were being taken out of the equation so as to not leave any living witnesses.

Which didn't bode well for Amanda, Brandon, or any of the other kidnapped victims from that original prison location. Kerrick worried about the well-being of those other victims now. While Kerrick's new organization had tracked those victims to their new prison, were they still alive at this very moment? His new employer was taking care of that element with a separate team of men. Kerrick understood the viability of compartmentalization in any op, but … hell. He had a vested interest and wanted continued updates on all aspects of this mission.

Even worse, how many other kidnap operations were active, just involving these lowlifes? He didn't even want to consider how many other separate criminal elements out there were responsible for other such kidnappings.

Maybe Mr. Coleman, Brandon's father, was dead, either as a witness or maybe as a willing partner in all this. Kerrick still awaited more information regarding his own damn op.

His phone beeped in his pocket, and, while he drove, he pulled it out and speed-read the text.

Brandon piped up, "You shouldn't text and drive."

He glanced into the rearview mirror and said, "You're right. I shouldn't." He dropped the phone beside him, but he'd already seen the message. His assistants had identified two of the faces on the gurneys that Griffin had supplied via his nighttime op immediately after rescuing Amanda and Brandon. One was the daughter of an opera singer and the other was the wife of a billionaire from Saudi Arabia.

To Kerrick, this seemed to be a pure blackmail scheme, just extorting money from the rich families so the kidnappers would return their loved ones relatively unharmed. Like a stream of income to fund the bad guys' main objective: the illegal harvesting of body parts.

Yet Amanda's kidnapping was to force her to divulge her cancer cure. And Brandon? While a brilliant kid, he seemed to be collateral damage for whatever his father had been up to. Kerrick wanted to ask his associates in his chat window if this was a working theory on their end too but knew that they would be heads down, already involved in doing their own research as well. Better to leave them alone to do what they do.

He and Griffin and their two special *packages* were long past the time frame when they were expected at the new safe house. But he and his partner had chosen not to share with anybody their actual whereabouts. Not now. Not yet. And the three people back at the first safe house seemed to know about the next safe house location, and that was too many people "in the know" for Kerrick.

Griffin had scouted out another location. Hence all the phone calls he had been making, including one to Delta, his old buddy, thinking he might give some updates that the others weren't willing to do. No such luck.

Up ahead was a fast-food place. Kerrick glanced into the back seat and asked, "Brandon, are you hungry?"

"Always," Brandon piped up. He looked out his window, saw the burger joint, and cried out, "Yes! Fries."

Kerrick pulled in and parked. Then he said, "We might as well all go in."

Griffin tore his attention from his phone and put it away, looking surprised.

Kerrick shrugged and said, "We could all use a chance to get out and to stretch our legs."

With everyone out, Kerrick glanced into the back seat of the car and pointed. "Is that yours, Brandon?"

It was a small pad of paper and a pen. Brandon nodded and dove into the back seat, then grabbed it up.

In a low tone, Kerrick told Amanda, "Don't leave anything in the car."

After giving him a quizzical glance, she nodded and cast a quick look into the back seat and nodded.

Griffin had pulled their stuff from the trunk. With a backpack each and a duffel bag at their sides, the two men walked in with everything they had into the restaurant. They led the way inside, and Kerrick didn't make any attempt to hide his face from any security cameras either.

He didn't care at this point, as he needed a few minutes to change vehicles. And that meant they had to exit one vehicle in order to get in the next one. They chose a booth at the far back, and he and Griffin stowed their gear at their feet. Once done, Griffin kept on walking. He called back as he headed for the men's room, "Order me a coffee."

Kerrick nodded. Knew Griffin from their previous time

in the navy. And the man was a master at finding new vehicles. As the waitress walked over with a big smile on her face, she asked if they wanted menus.

Brandon piped up. "I want a big burger with fries, no pickles," he announced without any warning.

Kerrick chuckled. "I guess that means two burgers for him for sure. And I'll need another two as well." Then he looked at Amanda. "What would you like, honey?"

As if understanding to keep it in the spirit of a family outing, she smiled at him and said, "I'd love a bowl of soup and a salad." The waitress immediately rattled off the soup of the day, and Amanda nodded. "That would be good."

Then the waitress asked Kerrick, "Anything else?"

He smiled and said, "Got any sandwiches to-go?"

"We have big sub sandwiches," she said. "I could make up a few of those for you."

He thought about it and then said, "Make four, please."

She nodded and disappeared in the back.

Amanda then glanced at Kerrick. "What about Griffin?"

"We'll get something to-go for him," he said.

Brandon looked at them, from one adult to the other, and then shook his head. "He shouldn't be that long in the bathroom."

"No," Kerrick announced. "And we can't be that long either. Hopefully the service here is very fast."

Not only was it fast but the food came piping hot, and it was good.

Kerrick bit into his burger and watched as Brandon very carefully laid his tomato off to the side and placed it just so on his napkin. Kerrick hadn't remembered him doing that the last time, but then the kid had been starving. Once he started to eat though, he didn't slow down, and he plowed through both burgers and all the fries. He kept looking at Kerrick's fries too.

Kerrick shook his head. "My fries, buddy."

At the crestfallen look Brandon gave him, Kerrick lifted his plate and dumped one-third of his fries onto Brandon's plate. Brandon quickly polished those off too. By the time they were gone, he still looked hungry.

When Kerrick got up and walked over to pay for the bill, he found their sub sandwiches waiting and also saw an apple pie sitting under the glass counter. "How much is the pie?"

"If they're cooked and ready to go, I sell them by the piece," she said. "But I do have a cooked spare, if you want one to take with you."

"Absolutely," he said. "And do you have any more of those fries? That kid's empty to his toes."

She chuckled. "Just a minute." Then she walked around into the back, pulled out a cardboard carryout container, and completely stuffed it full of fries. After putting a lid on it and putting it in a bag, she handed it to Brandon. "There you go, big guy. Eat up."

His face lit up the room as he cried out, "Thanks."

Kerrick asked Amanda, "Do we need anything else, honey?"

"Water," she said. Amanda took the bag with the sandwiches and the pie, then walked to the cooler and grabbed several water bottles.

"Good idea. I should have thought of that. Plus a couple coffees to-go for me for the road," he said. "Amanda, do you want one?"

"Yes, please," she said.

He ordered two more coffees to-go and said, "It's a long trip." The woman behind the counter just laughed, filled their order, and totaled their bill. Kerrick paid, and they headed outside with their food and drinks.

Arms now ladened, they walked around the side of the building, as if they'd parked there. Kerrick knew exactly how this worked, but Amanda and Brandon looked at him in confusion. Their vehicle was gone. As Kerrick walked farther down the side of the building, he spotted Griffin on his phone—of course—sitting in the cab of a big jacked-up F-250 pickup. Kerrick opened the passenger side, set down the groceries, putting the coffee on the floorboard so it was safely stowed. Brandon was superexcited about the pickup, but it was so high up he could hardly climb in, needing some help from Kerrick. Even Amanda needed a hand to get into the back. But, once they were all loaded up, Kerrick looked at Griffin and said, "How much food do you need?"

Griffin shrugged. "One of those sandwiches will do. Unless you only ordered enough for the three of you."

But Brandon popped up from the back and said, "I have a lot of fries for you."

Kerrick was amused at his generosity. Brandon ripped off the top of the cardboard box, split up the fries, and handed the bigger half forward for Griffin.

Pleased, Griffin smiled at him and said, "Thanks, Brandon. That was thoughtful of you."

"Only because I'm already full," Brandon said, munching away on his own fries.

Griffin gave a shout of laughter and pulled the pickup out of the restaurant's rear parking lot. Then they circled around to hit the highway going in the opposite direction.

Brandon cried out, "I know this area."

"What do you mean, you know this area?" Kerrick asked, sure the alarm in his tone was evident to all. "Have you ever been to that café before?"

"No," he said, "but coming down the left"—and he pointed out a bunch of buildings that looked like old farmhouses—"I've been there before."

"Why and what for?"

"With my father. He's got some friends down there."

"Do you know how to get home from here?"

Brandon screwed up his face and then nodded. "I think so, yes." Then he fired off directions, which made sense somewhat.

Kerrick could see these details came from the total-recall part of Brandon's brain. On a hunch, Kerrick had Griffin follow the kid's instructions for the next twenty minutes, trying to see if they would find out where Brandon lived. When they came down a residential street, Brandon said, "This is close but not quite."

Kerrick turned to look at him. "So we're in the right area?"

Brandon stared around, mystified. "We are, but I think we're like a block over." He looked ahead and saw a popular ice cream place and cried out, "Yes! I've been to that one." He quickly adjusted his directions, and, before long, they drove down a street no longer filled with middle-class homes. In fact, it was in a commercial district with a lot of warehouses but heading toward the lower end of the business class.

"So is this where your home is or where your father works?"

"Both," he said. "He lives and does his business from home."

"The selling of the body organs?" Amanda asked, worried. Her gaze kept going around the area.

Brandon nodded. "We live up top."

"That can't be very nice," Kerrick mentioned.

"You get used to seeing dead bodies all the time," he said with a shrug. "We're organic organisms, so it's not like it makes a difference."

"I guess."

They drove down the road slower now, giving Brandon time to process his surroundings, when he called out and leaned forward between the two men in the front seat. "Stop."

Griffin pulled off to the side of the road and asked, "What are we looking at?"

"That building in the front of the warehouse on the next block? That blue one? That's home."

Kerrick looked at him and whispered, "Was it always burned up like that?"

Brandon shook his head slowly, fear on his face as he whispered, "No. That's new."

# CHAPTER 12

THE PAIN IN Brandon's voice broke Amanda's heart. This kid had lost so much so recently and had been so stalwart for so long. She gently massaged his back. "We don't know if your father was in there," she said reassuringly. "He could be fine."

Brandon stared at the building with a haunted look on his face. "No, but it wouldn't surprise me. That was arson."

"Your dad has some pretty big enemies, correct?"

"Yes," Brandon said in a small voice. "He's in a bad business, and he has a lot of bad friends."

"I'm sorry," Amanda said. She looked at the two men. "Is there any point in going inside and checking it out?"

"I think we need to," Kerrick said. He glanced back at Brandon. "Should I take a closer look at any particular part of the building?"

Brandon shrugged and said, "The offices, especially the back wall on the right side, but Dad had a safe in his bedroom, above the office. He also had a fire escape out the back, so maybe he got out safely." He looked into the faces of the three adults with him, some hope creeping into his expression. "Like we did when we left the motel."

Kerrick studied the extent of the burn. Not a whole lot of the outside shell remained, but the fire looked like it had been stopped midburn. Who was the arsonist? That wasn't his job right now, but he was curious. Still, to cover his tracks, Mr. Coleman might have set it himself.

Kerrick glanced at Griffin and said, "I'll get out. You take them around the block a couple times." And without giving anybody a chance to argue, he exited the pickup and disappeared into the closest building on this block, another warehouse.

Amanda leaned forward and asked Griffin, "What's the point in getting out here and going into a building right beside us?"

Griffin smiled at her. "It's not for you to wonder why."

"Well, you can't quote poetry to me and expect to shut me up here," she said in exasperation. "He's out there alone. This could be dangerous."

"Exactly," Griffin said. "Which is why he told me to drive you around the block, so that you two don't look like you're a party to any of this." And, on that note, he pulled back into the street and headed down the block. As they drove past the scorched building, he slowed slightly so they could stare at it. She could still see the second floor was largely intact, but nobody appeared to be around, and no windows were left. And, if it hadn't been ramshackled beforehand, it would have been well and truly looted by now.

KERRICK MADE IT to the edge of the burned-up building without seeing anybody—or anybody seeing him. He quickly moved down what was left of one side of the building, just to make a quick first-pass inspection, hating the acid-burn smell emanating from it. Had anybody even come to take a look at what was inside this building after the fire had died down? He saw freezers and cold storage units, but none of those would be powered at this point.

What happened to the "perishable goods" that Mr. Coleman kept? Kerrick hated to think that body parts were still in there. Yet it was all too possible. No way would he open one to confirm. He'd leave that to the authorities. Or to Mr. Coleman.

Holding his T-shirt over his nose to keep from inhaling too much of the acidic smell inside, Kerrick stepped into the charred building and walked through carefully. Everything here was black and crispy, like it had been fried at high temperatures. Back toward the smaller rooms, the offices, however, there was much less damage, as if the fire had begun in the front area and had burned backward.

He checked out the biggest office and the charred desk but didn't see very much. Singed papers were atop the filing cabinet, but he found no computers or electronics. But then, why would there be? Somebody else would have been here before him, either taking the electronics before starting the fire or the locals had cleared out anything worth pawning after the fire.

The wooden stairs going up to the second floor were badly damaged, but the metal fire escape outside looked like a viable option. He quickly scooted up the ladder and made his way inside, then stopped. Most of the flooring was gone, leaving only the rafters. The bedroom perimeter was still intact, but its contents were quite badly charred. The bed itself had caught fire. He should have asked Brandon where the safe was. He pulled out his phone and called Griffin to ask Brandon.

**Inset into the wall near the fire escape but on the**

**outside exterior wall.**

From where he stood, he looked, then took two careful steps, to where the safe supposedly was. Enough of the wall had burned away that he caught a glimpse of black metal. If the safe was still intact, still locked, then anybody who knew it was here hadn't come back to empty it yet. Probably waiting to make sure the fire was completely out. Or to hire a safecracker. The other option was that the safe was empty to begin with.

He took one step closer, carefully balancing on the rafters, and bent down, peeling off the wallboard. The safe itself was small and would be easy to remove from the studs around it now since they were badly charred. It took a few moments longer to completely uncover the safe. The combination lock was still secured. He couldn't open it safely here as he didn't trust the rafter he stood on, but the safe was small enough that he could carry it.

With it securely under his arm, he made his way back down the fire escape and headed around the back corner to meet up with the rest of them. As soon as the pickup pulled alongside him, he hopped inside, and they drove away.

Brandon leaned over and asked, in a hushed tone, "You took the whole safe?"

"The wall was damaged enough that it was easier to remove the whole thing than to take the time to open it there."

"Can you open it?" Amanda asked.

"I hope so," he said, studying the front of the safe. "It's not really that complicated. Without Brandon's personal knowledge of its location, finding it would have been more complicated. Without that tip, if it hadn't been for the fire, it wouldn't have been easy to find the safe at all." He quickly said something about cracking the combination code. It took him four minutes and thirty seconds to open the safe.

Griffin laughed at him. "You should have had that done in under four minutes," he teased Kerrick.

Kerrick shot him a look. "If we weren't driving around corners like madmen, I would have." He slowly dug inside to find it full of bookkeeping ledgers and cash.

Brandon whistled long and hard. "That's a lot of moo-lah."

Kerrick nodded slowly. "It is. So why didn't your father come back for it?" He twisted to look at Brandon.

And Brandon looked at him and sniffled once.

Kerrick nodded. "Because you know and I know that, if there was any way he could have, your father would have come back to get this, wouldn't he?"

Brandon slowly nodded.

Kerrick glanced at Griffin and said, "You and I need to analyze what's in these ledgers. We'll probably need your help, Brandon. I'm sorry, but it's not looking good for your father."

"Which also would explain why nobody had put out the word that Brandon was missing," Amanda said. "Because your father would have done that too, if he could, right?" she asked Brandon.

Brandon sniffled again, nodding his head.

"True enough," Griffin added.

While Kerrick pulled out the money, he roughly count-ed it, noting at least ten but possibly upward of twenty thousand US dollars in bundles here, but there were also bundles of different currencies. With the ledgers open, he checked to see if anything else suspicious could be found at first glance.

Inside one were passports for Brandon and for Mr.

Coleman, as well as other legal documents, like Brandon's birth certificate. Those were all good to have when leaving the country. And it appeared that Brandon's father intended to take Brandon with him. Kerrick showed Brandon his passport to help ease the boy's current pain.

Brandon grabbed it like a lifeline, tracing the small book in his hands, while Amanda wrapped an arm around him and pulled him closer.

With the ledgers on his lap, Kerrick quickly flipped through them, not understanding the codes for everything listed herein, codes using shorthand or acronyms to hide the real transactions. Maybe after Brandon had some time to deal with this, Kerrick might approach him for help with his dad's shorthand. A lot of money was involved. The other ledger held bank account info, security information, and listings of companies that Mr. Coleman had business dealings with. *That* was interesting.

At the top of the list was the company that Amanda worked for, that she held a major shareholder interest in— Scion Labs. He lifted it up for her to see. Had she not been involved in the kidnapping event herself, she would have been one major person of interest. Even now, investigators who didn't know her might still consider her involved in her own kidnapping.

When she sucked in her breath, he nodded and said, "And here is another link between Mr. Coleman and Scion Labs."

She sighed. "Besides Hinkleman kidnapping Mr. Coleman's own son and jailing him." She shook her head.

Brandon read off the name and turned to look at her. "Is that the company you work for?"

She sank into the back seat and nodded slowly. "It is,

indeed," she said faintly. "But I don't think we've ever bought body parts before."

"If you were doing business with my dad," Brandon said, "then you were. Or you could have been using the cadavers for further research. He was selling everything from cellular tissue to brain matter."

"It's possible that somebody doing research at Scion needed some cadaver tissue," she said. "We work on all different levels of the body's systems at different times."

"Yes, but dead bodies? How does that help you?" Kerrick asked.

"Scion is first and foremost a research facility, and examining a dead body that died from cancer or whatever does leave clues," she said, making excuses. "So I can't really say that it isn't possible that we dealt with Brandon's father or purchased body parts from him. It is quite likely possible that somebody was using your father's services. However, I don't imagine too many places would purchase these items."

"You mean, *legally*," Griffin said, his tone dry. They made several quick turns, and he pulled into an underground parking area. Once the gate opened, letting them through, he drove farther inside and then into a parking space marked with the number forty-two on it. He shut off the engine and said, "We're home."

"Whose home?" Brandon asked.

Griffin chuckled. "The driver of the lorry, that's who."

*The* dead *driver of the lorry*, Kerrick thought, feeling Amanda's stare along the back of his head, but he ignored her. He took the contents of the safe but left the safe behind, and, with the rest of the food and their gear, they hopped out of the pickup, locked it up, and went upstairs. He knew Griffin had made arrangements to get this apartment, one way or another.

Standing before door number forty-two, they didn't find any duplicate keys left behind in the expected hiding places. Not that Kerrick had expected as much, now that they were off-grid themselves. Griffin quickly picked the lock and let them in. He waited at the doorway with the other two while Kerrick made a quick search through the apartment, and then everybody came inside. He locked up after them.

The apartment was furnished in a contemporary style, more of a single-male variety than catering to that of a family. Brandon bounced through it, excited to see something new and different, including the furniture, which was pretty New Age stuff. As he danced around, he called out, "I like it."

Amanda looked like she was wilting. She went over to the nearest large recliner and sagged into the plushy softness.

Kerrick looked at her with worry. "Do you need a nap?"

"I'm okay still," she said. "I got a few hours last night, but don't want to ruin a good night tonight."

"Your body's still recovering," he said. "So, if you need to sleep, let us know."

"And what? Sleep in this *dead* guy's bed?" she whispered.

Kerrick looked at her and said, "It's necessary for the time being."

Her shoulders sagged, and she nodded. "I know. It doesn't mean I have to like it though."

"It's your company noted on that ledger ..." he reminded her.

"I know I didn't purchase anything from Brandon's father," she said. "But Hinkleman could have, as CEO of Scion. But did the board of directors know too? Or was Hinkleman just using his position for some off-the-books deals?"

Kerrick's face was grim. "That's what we need to find out."

She was silent as she pulled her knees to her chest and curled up in the big chair.

Immediately Brandon hopped over, snagged a blanket off one of the other chairs, and draped it over her. He gave her a pat on the shoulder. "You just sleep."

She chuckled and said, "What will you do?"

"I'll check out one of those sandwiches they brought."

She stared at him in disbelief, but Kerrick had heard it all and seen it all with young boys. They ate until they dropped in a food coma, like after a big Thanksgiving Day meal of seven courses. He brought the sandwiches into the kitchen, handing one to Brandon, then poked around to make sure there was coffee in this place, real coffee, and put on a pot. Griffin was once again on his phone.

Kerrick himself needed to check to see where they were at for further details, but it looked like there was more of a connection to her company than Amanda had fully realized. That had to be hard in itself. When he glanced back at her, her eyes were closed, and her chest rose and fell in a deep and steady motion. He next checked Brandon, who was watching her between bites of his sandwich.

"We'll let her sleep while she can," he cautioned.

Brandon nodded, swallowed. "I don't think she's having an easy time of this."

"And why is that?"

Brandon looked up at him, chewed a bit more, and smiled. "She's too much of an adult to not find the worry in this, and I'm too much of a child not to find the joy."

Talk about being old beyond his years. Kerrick stared at

the boy in astonishment, but Brandon just shrugged and attacked his sandwich. When the coffee was done dripping, Brandon had finished his sandwich, then skipped off to inspect the apartment further, while Kerrick took his coffee cup over to the kitchen table, set up his laptop and his notepad, and sat down to get to work. He would require more sleep himself, but he needed to sort out with Griffin the roster for their security shifts.

They couldn't stay here for too long, and he wasn't sure if Griffin had made actual arrangements with the apartment management or was just taking advantage. Either way, they were doing what they needed to stay safe. At least, until tomorrow, when they could arrange for another location. Only one night per each. As he checked out his emails, the mysterious but helpful chat box opened. Kerrick decided to call it the Mavericks chat box now, due to their unfettered approach to justice. He read the new message.

**Where are you?**
**New place.**
**Where?**
**Outside of town.**

He wasn't sure why he was being evasive, but, so far, he hadn't exactly had any reason to trust anybody.

**You were supposed to be at a safe house.**
**Didn't feel right.**

Silence came first. **Okay.**

He gave a nod at that. "Damn right. The reason you hired me," he muttered, "is because my instincts are solid. And nothing about this case feels right. In fact, it's all gone to hell."

# CHAPTER 13

BY MIDAFTERNOON THEY had settled into Stanley's apartment, their newest safe house. Brandon had crashed on the couch, still sound asleep. Griffin was on the floor on the carpet just in front of him, protecting the boy even while asleep, whereas both Kerrick and Amanda sat at the kitchen table. She cast her mind back to the day when she had been kidnapped. If she had realized it had been Dr. Hinkleman right from the beginning, it would have made a lot more sense. He hadn't shown up to work on that Friday before. He had been very controlling, hovering over everyone's work recently—more so than normal. So missing a normal workday without any explanation was unusual.

"What are you thinking so heavily about?" Kerrick asked, his tone low.

She glanced at the other two, still sleeping soundly, and whispered, "Those two look good together."

"I was thinking the same thing," Kerrick said, "while I watched over you and Brandon early this morning."

She glanced at him. "It's the first time you've mentioned that, holding me close as I fought my own demons."

His smile was gentle but filled with understanding. "We all have demons, and it's no shame in wanting to be held. It's a human comfort we all need from time to time."

"Well, thank you for that and for continuing to look

after us."

He shrugged. "Honestly, I'm not sure what to do with you."

She stared at him in astonishment.

He flashed her a wicked grin. "Other than the usual things a man might want to share with a woman."

She flushed. "I don't think so."

"Are you sure?" he teased. "According to my file, you haven't had a boyfriend since your ex."

She rolled her eyes at him. "So what? And that doesn't mean I haven't hooked up during that time, although that's hardly a replacement for a real relationship."

He shook his head. "Absolutely it's not, but it doesn't mean we can't have both. Besides anyone can see we're attracted to each other. That's not something to ignore."

She stared at him again in shock. "Where's this coming from, all of a sudden?"

"I'm not sure, honestly." He shrugged. "But, ever since I saw your picture, I couldn't get you out of my mind. And then there's the fact that I admire you very much. Well, that's the best basis I know for a relationship."

"Wow." She didn't even know what to say. Her heart knew how to feel though as it warmed to the idea in a big way. She sat back and smirked at him. "Do you always fall in love with women's pictures?"

"Well, I wouldn't go that far," he said, chuckling. "But I do appreciate what you've been doing with your research, and I admire how you've handled yourself since the kidnapping. You got yourself out of a really sticky situation, and you rescued the boy too."

At the mention of Brandon, she glanced over at him, and her smile fell away. "What happens to him if his father's dead?"

"I don't know how that works here," he said quietly. "There will be a system in place, but I can't even begin to guess what that is."

She nodded slowly. "And generally I live in Paris. But I really would like to talk to my father." She smiled. "He has a place in England," she said. "Just a little coastal holiday home, where we used to meet up for holidays. Loved those times."

He stared at her in surprise.

"I was hoping to come over and spend a couple weeks there this year. I just could never find the time."

"A workaholic," he said with a nod.

"I highly doubt you're any different," she said with a chuckle.

"Not so sure about that," he said. "I was at a crossroads myself, trying to figure out where and what I would do next—when I got the call to come rescue you."

"You're not Special Forces?"

"I am, in a way," he said, "but I was a Navy SEAL before. It was time for a switch."

He didn't go into all the details, and she respected his privacy too much to ask. Most likely he couldn't answer either way. But her insides felt pretty warm and fuzzy that he had opened up about how he felt about her. "How is this a switch?" she asked with a note of humor.

"Well, I'm not on a ship, for one."

"Too bad," she said. "I wouldn't mind being on one. The water always soothes my soul."

He stopped and stared at her, one eyebrow raised. "And that's a good idea too." He considered the small apartment around him. "That could be our next step."

She frowned at him. "And what exactly would that next step be?"

"Let me think about it," he said. "It wouldn't work for long, but you'd certainly be safe."

Just then a hard rap came at the apartment door.

All laughter fell from his face. He held up a finger and rose from the kitchen table. Her heart pounding, she dashed to hide beside the fridge. Griffin was already up on his feet, moving smoothly and lightly, picking up Brandon and ducking into one of the bedrooms. She wished she could go with him.

When the pounding came again, a voice called out, "Kerrick!"

Swearing gently, Kerrick opened the door and let somebody in.

"What the hell's going on?" the man asked.

"I didn't like the safe house alternatives," Kerrick snapped. "I do what I do because of my instincts. And my instincts said that other plan sucked."

That brought the stranger up short. He glanced around and said, "Where are they?"

Something about Kerrick's attitude had her stepping back a little bit farther behind the fridge as Kerrick answered, "They're safe."

"Are they here with you?"

"No," he said. "Griffin's got them."

"Shit."

She could just barely see the stranger as he ran his fingers through his hair. "I'll have to fix this."

"Fix what?"

"This." And he turned and stormed from the apartment.

Kerrick slowly closed the door behind him and locked it.

She stepped around the corner and asked, "Who was that?"

"I'm not exactly sure," Kerrick said. "Most of the men I work with in this group are strangers."

Griffin stepped forward from the back and said, "That was Delta."

Kerrick looked at him and said, "Seriously?"

Griffin nodded. "He's a friend of mine."

"Well, he's a rattled friend now," Amanda said curiously. "You guys don't even know who you work with?"

"We each know someone from our past," Kerrick said. "And Griffin and I know each other obviously, but we don't necessarily know who all else is in the team at any given time."

"Yeah, I got that, what with the Greek letters of the alphabet for designations instead of real names. I'd be hard-pressed to trust people without their real names too." She shook her head. "He didn't sound happy that you're here. And how did he know we *were* here?"

Kerrick stared at her and said, "I was just trying to figure that out." He looked again at Griffin. "Did you give them a heads-up?"

Griffin shook his head. "No."

"Are you tracked?"

Griffin shook his head again. "Better not be." He stared at Kerrick and asked, "You?"

"No, not that I know of." Then he frowned, studied the rest of them, and said, "But that's the only way they would know." He stared at Griffin. "It must be our disposable phones." Then he froze. "No. They can track us through the Mavericks chat window." He swore. "I should have thought of that."

"It makes sense though. They are the ones we keep asking for intel."

"*Mavericks* chat window?" Amanda asked, her lips quirking at the corners.

Kerrick gave her a silly grin and shrugged. "I coined the term. But the Mavericks is our code name."

"*Mavericks* works for me," Griffin said. "I like it." His grin was huge, and a mischievous gleam was in his gaze.

"You two may be mavericks, but you're still the good guys."

"Well, maybe we do need to sneak into France and see what we can come up with."

"About what?" Amanda asked.

"More information on Hinkleman and the purchase of body parts by the Scion Labs company, whether Hinkleman acted alone or in concert with the company, whether Hinkleman or Scion were involved in both ends of the body-parts transactions," Kerrick said, watching as Amanda's face contorted more and more at each theory.

"Oh, my God. You don't think … Would my company tell you the truth? Even if they weren't involved, would you believe them?" she asked in exasperation.

"That's why we need to check them out more closely," Griffin added.

"Wait a minute. … At work, that last Friday I was there, I overhead a conversation about Scion's big research vessel being off the coast of Norway. How most of the Scion people would be there soon. Or should be there right now. For some conference."

"On a research vessel?"

She nodded.

The two men looked at each other, their gazes intent, as

if sorting their way through this.

"We'd have to get across the water without leaving a trail, without alerting anybody at Scion," Kerrick noted, to himself mostly.

"I don't understand," she said. "Unless your bags, any of our clothing, or our persons are being tracked by Hinkleman or his goons, how else would they know where we are when we leave here?"

"Satellite," Griffin stated. "Traffic cams."

"We still have to sort out what's going on with the UK kidnapping ring and the fact that everything seems tied to France and now Norway, what with that Norwegian research ship and your father living in Norway and most of Scion Labs' France-based employees, your coworkers, gathering there too. It makes me nervous, but I also wonder if we should be on that ship too."

She snorted. "Good luck with that. It's massive, but, regardless of space and accommodations, it's not like those invitations are just handed out."

"So what kind of conference is going on?" he asked, slowly turning to look at her.

"I don't really know," she said. "I was going to check into it further, but then my life went sideways. I thought, as a board member and a major shareholder and one of their top researchers, that I would have been invited, but I wasn't."

"Maybe Hinkleman had something to do with that?" Griffin said. Then he frowned. "I agree, Kerrick. I think we need to catch a ride."

Kerrick nodded. "I was thinking that too. We could pull the secret card."

Griffin snorted. "How many times had we just boarded

a ship before moving out on a new mission, leaving in silence?"

"Often," Kerrick said with a smirk. "No reason we can't do it again."

Griffin's eyes lit up at that idea. "Let me see who's close by." And he turned and headed to his laptop. Before he typed anything, he added, "I'm using my own computer. It's been swept and not out of my sight."

Kerrick turned toward Amanda. "We'll be on the move soon. You should crash now, while you can."

She slowly shook her head. "I'm not sure I can. All of a sudden, you're talking about how we have to get onto this research vessel. I don't even think that's possible. Or are you thinking that you and Griffin would go, leaving me and Brandon stashed somewhere?" When she saw the truth acknowledged in his eyes, she shook her head. "Hell, no. Brandon, yes. But me, no."

"You're not leaving me behind," Brandon shouted. He came out of the bedroom and raced toward Amanda, throwing his arms around her waist. She wrapped him up tight in her arms.

"Everybody can't go," Kerrick said. "More chances of us being caught. Someone could recognize Amanda. A blond female stands out. And way too dangerous a situation to bring a child into."

"Dangerous on a research ship? For some meeting?" Brandon argued, but he faced Amanda.

Kerrick just stared at her and waited. She filtered through what Kerrick had said, and then she slowly sighed. "Is there another ship we can stay on while you guys head out there?"

He flashed a grin. "Maybe. Depends."

She glared at him, and he shrugged and said, "I can't answer that yet."

She looked down at Brandon. "We'll have to leave soon. Can you go back to sleep?"

He immediately shook his head. "No, I can't. I'm hungry again."

She shook her head, then just raised her hands in surrender and said, "There are still a few leftovers."

A couple sandwiches remained. She put one on a plate and handed it to him as he sat at the table and promptly scoffed it up. She turned when she heard Griffin and Kerrick whispering behind her and glared at them. "Now what?"

But they were setting their watches and talking about buying new phones. "I'll be right back," Griffin said walking to the door.

"We're leaving soon," Kerrick said with a smile to both Amanda and Brandon. "So be ready."

"I've been nothing but ready," she snapped. "I, however, don't even have a change of clothes."

"Well, we have to get you some interim gear," he said, looking at Griffin, who nodded in return. "It won't be fancy though."

Griffin promptly left, only to return in an hour, distributing one new cell phone to each of them, including Brandon, with strict instructions to not use them unless their life depended on it. That 9-1-1 calls were allowed, as long as they were no longer than thirty seconds in duration. "I've keyed in one new cell number into these phones. For Amanda, it's Kerrick's. For Brandon, it's Amanda's. Dial that number if you get lost and keep it close."

Amanda and Brandon nodded.

"I mean it, Brandon. Your life is at stake here, so you

must do as we say. Or you lose this privilege. Do you understand?" Kerrick asked.

"Sure. Got it."

"Your life and Amanda's life too." Kerrick stared at the boy, who nodded and stared at Amanda with a very serious look on his face. Kerrick could only hope he truly understood how serious this was. "No calls to your father for either of you. Understand?"

Amanda and Brandon nodded again.

When everyone agreed to these terms, the guys made their calls. She sat here and waited until they were done, her fingers thrumming on the tabletop. But she smiled at Brandon and said, "If nothing else, we'll have an exciting adventure."

Brandon immediately bobbed his head, his mouth full of sandwich. "I hope we get to go on one of those big naval warships. That would be awesome."

She stared at him, then glanced up at the two men, and wondered just what they had planned. She hoped it wasn't a naval ship. That sounded noisy and crowded. And she didn't think they would blend in very easily, particularly not a child on a naval vessel—not even a woman on a navy ship, not even in 2019—hence the problem with her and Brandon going aboard a military ship. Maybe it *was* better if they stayed on land. Only she didn't want to be separated from any of them.

ONE OF THE last calls Kerrick made had been to the Mavericks organization. They had been more efficient than Kerrick had expected once his request had gone out and plans were made. He told them that they were leaving in four hours but they were on the road in thirty minutes—in a new vehicle compliments of Griffin. They hit the coastline late that afternoon and boarded a small ship heading out toward the deeper waters. This particular ship was known for moving people in the dark of night. A contact he planned to keep for future reference.

For now, they moved in broad daylight; night would fall before they reached their destination.

As for Amanda and Brandon, they were both dressed in black. Amanda's hair had been covered with a soft fishing cap. Brandon sat by her side. He had promised to always stay within arm's reach of Amanda, and that promise was something he took very seriously.

Kerrick turned to face the ocean, closing his eyes and lifting his face into the breeze. The waves were a bit choppy but not enough to slow their schedule.

He stood at the front of the boat, letting the pilot cross the water as hard and as fast as the boat would go. He turned back and motioned at Amanda and Brandon to go down below. She nodded and led the boy underneath. She shot Kerrick a special smile and a little finger wave as the two of them tucked up into one of the big bunks underneath. He smiled, caught Griffin's raised eyebrows, and then shrugged as he turned around.

His sea legs were something he never lost. The water was his element. It didn't matter whether he was in the water or on a boat like now. On any water vessel, he felt at home. He stood here for a long moment, his mind formulating the next step of the plan. Griffin tapped him on the shoulder. He turned, and Griffin motioned toward the back of the boat, where they could sit and talk.

As he sat down, Griffin said, "I have the location of the research ship." He held out his phone to show him.

Kerrick looked at the map Griffin had and pulled out his laptop. Kerrick brought up real-time photos. "And our ship is where?"

Griffin enlarged the map, so they could see the red dot showing their destination. They would transfer to a helicopter sometime after they arrived there, which would take them to the USS *Antietam*, which was even closer to Norway. Kerrick was fine with that. They had avoided any street cams so far. The satellites? Well, … they all had on some kind of a hat, so their faces had been covered somewhat. That would hinder any facial recognition software from getting a valid hit. He hoped …

Now it was just a hop, skip, and a jump from the *Antietam* to the research vessel. It would have been easier and faster to fly straight into Norway and then catch a ride out to the Scion ship. But this way, they didn't leave a paper trail, and nobody at Scion had a clue what they were doing or even who they were.

They traveled for hours before the pilot called to Kerrick. He looked up to see the majestic carrier before them, lighting up the dark evening and the darker ocean. They pulled up slowly to it, next to the affixed ladder on its side, where the four of them would disembark. It was a long way up the side of this navy transport. These ships easily stood one hundred feet tall, just the part sitting atop the water, but a landing was not too far up its side where Brandon and Amanda must get to.

Kerrick quickly woke them up, and, as they shook the sleep out of their gazes, he told them how this would work. He would usher them over the side of this small boat, where they must climb up a ladder on the huge ship, with Kerrick ahead of them and Griffin behind them—to make sure they didn't fall and to navigate them successfully into the cargo levels within.

Brandon's jaw dropped as he stared around. He whispered, "This is huge."

Kerrick placed a finger on his lips and whispered, "From here on in, not a word. Not until you reach your quarters, all right?"

BRANDON'S GAZE WIDENED again, and he quickly nodded. Amanda wrapped an arm around the kid's shoulders and tucked him up closer to her as they got into line. She was cursing her own lack of fitness by the time they climbed the ladder and stepped onto a landing. Brandon made the climb much more easily.

One navy officer met them, led them through a series of steps up and down, and then filed them into one small room. In all that time, not one word had been spoken. As soon as they were inside, Kerrick motioned to the bunk on the bottom and said softly, "That's for you two."

Amanda nodded, laid down, and urged in low voice, "Brandon, come lie down with me."

Immediately he hopped into the bed beside her and curled up tight. Kerrick grabbed a blanket by her feet and threw it over them. "One of us will always be here," he murmured. "But no talking. If you have to, whisper."

Griffin sat down on the small bench space opposite them. As soon as Amanda closed her eyes, Kerrick smacked Griffin lightly on the shoulder and said, "I'll be back soon."

Then he disappeared.

KERRICK HEADED BACK onto the landing where they had come from, having memorized his path easily. There, he met the one person who had helped him off the boat and into the ship's belly. The hired boat they'd arrived on was long gone.

Kerrick was handed an envelope. He nodded, opened it up, quickly took a look. He checked the time; they were leaving in six hours. With a pat on his buddy's shoulder, Kerrick returned to their room. By the time he got there, Amanda and Brandon were sound asleep, and Griffin was working on his computer. Kerrick stepped inside, closed the door carefully so that he didn't wake anybody, and dropped the envelope beside Griffin. "Helicopter out in six hours," he said.

Griffin nodded. "Perfect." Then the man glanced at Brandon. "He'll need food before then."

"He'll get it." Kerrick shrugged. "Meals will be delivered."

Griffin nodded. "Secrecy at all costs. Still, I think we should have left them on shore."

"I wish," he said. "But there's just the two of us, so who were we to leave them with?"

Griffin winced. "I know. That's why they're still with us."

"Any news on the other kidnappers?"

"The Mavericks have a location pinpointed," Griffin said in a low voice. "Already setting up a sting operation to get in."

"Good," Kerrick said. "I don't understand exactly what

the bottom line is here with the company, Scion Labs. What does it seek to gain? To think they were holding Amanda and Brandon under those conditions is beyond belief."

"Our guys might have found Brandon's father," Griffin said, his voice dropping even lower. But his tone told Kerrick so much.

"They found him in the warehouse?"

He nodded. "Crispy critter, no ID on him, and no way to know for sure. But it's highly suspected that's who he is."

"I hate results like that," Kerrick muttered. "We need one hundred percent ID."

"I agree. We can send over some DNA."

"We could, but they should have enough to confirm Mr. Coleman's DNA via Brandon's DNA found on his body tracker."

"Exactly," Griffin said. Then he waited a heartbeat and added, "But that wasn't mentioned."

"That's *not* good news." Kerrick's gaze flew to meet his partner's. "An oversight? Haven't gotten to it yet? My gut's talking to me." He brought out a phone and quickly asked.

He read out the almost immediate response. "DNA was too degraded to match."

"Convenient for the killer." The two men frowned at each other.

Griffin said, sending a wary look to Kerrick. "But, ever since meeting up with that threesome … that's why we switched out that next safe house, why we left our Mavericks-issued phones behind. Something there wasn't right. At least we have a secure connection to the Maverick team. They can track us. But we don't want Hinkleman's goons doing so."

Kerrick sat here, pondering that further. "But *Brandon*?"

"Might have been kidnapped to keep his father in line. Particularly if Mr. Coleman was supplying the Scion Labs company with his very specialized products, which Coleman's ledger seems to indicate. Then killed when he wouldn't cooperate? Or Brandon's father faked his own death? It's not like he wouldn't have access to a body as a substitute?"

"So, no political ties that we know of, but a potentially worldwide service industry that Amanda's kidnappers, that Scion Labs, needed?" Kerrick nodded slowly. "God, this could be so much bigger than just those three holding facilities we know of in London. I mean, illegal organ harvesting brings to mind kidnapping, human trafficking, just to kill them for their organs. The legal version would hardly be pretty, except for the intended end result—saving a person's life. Otherwise, it would be a damn ugly business if Mr. Coleman were illegally harvesting."

"The question is," Griffin began, "whether he wanted to stop doing it or whether they were looking for something a little more unusual."

"Are you talking about illegally harvesting stem cells?"

The room went quiet.

There was absolutely nothing good about that line of thought. If Brandon's father dealt in legal donations of human organs, that was one thing. Kerrick could only hope that the people donating their body parts were dead from natural causes. But what if Brandon's dad had been requested by the kidnappers—aka Scion Labs—to find a particular body part? Of course with a matching blood type, to use in black-market organ transplant surgeries. Or, in properly matched human volunteers, for those human trials that Amanda needs to prove her cure, which were so hard to get official permission for.

Regardless of which purpose, maybe Scion had placed too many orders for organs or cadavers not currently in stock at Mr. Coleman's?

Or was this ultimately about finding the more universal body part: stem cells that grew into various other body parts? And in numbers that Brandon's dad couldn't foresee supplying in normal legal situations. That would certainly be a valid reason to hold his son hostage and, once Brandon escaped, to then burn down Mr. Coleman's warehouse with him in it. "We have to get onto the research vessel," Kerrick said.

"Well, we're getting there, just another hop, skip and a jump away. At least they're having an exciting adventure," Griffin said, with a nod to their sleeping companions. "Brandon's quite the character."

Kerrick nodded, but he kept quiet.

"And you and Amanda seem to have hit it off," Griffin pushed.

"What's not to like? She's nice. I admire her strength, resourcefulness, and especially the fact that she's a brainiac and doing something worthwhile with it. Obviously it's easy to respect her for that too."

"Well, I saw an awful lot of heat and sparks between you two that had nothing to do with respect and admiration," Griffin said, chuckling. "But that's all right. You're entitled to your privacy."

"I wish," Kerrick said. "As you know we have had no privacy."

"I know. … I was really surprised to hear you were in."

"Ditto."

The two men looked at each other, taking their measure.

"Are you staying in?" Griffin asked.

"I'm not sure. I wasn't expecting this at all," he said. "This opportunity that arose." Then he studied Griffin and asked, "You?"

Griffin nodded. "Same. Although I'm not sure that I was quite as ready as you to leave the navy. The SEALs team that I worked with was great. But you get to the point where you wake up in the morning and wonder when it's enough."

"Exactly," Kerrick said. "And this seemed like something worthwhile that I could move on to."

"Exactly," Griffin said. "You'll do more?"

Kerrick snorted. "Got to survive this one first."

"I'm surprised, given the sophistication of this kidnapping operation, how they have obviously done this before," Griffin said slowly, "that we haven't been attacked. In my head, there were a couple opportunities where the local goons could have taken us out."

Kerrick stared at his buddy, his mind going back over everything they had encountered so far. "Well, I could confirm one opportunity. Potentially a second one, yes. The fact that they haven't is interesting, isn't it?"

"And dangerous," Griffin said. "I can't help but think it's a trap."

"The research ship itself? Or every step of the way getting there?"

"The vessel," he said slowly. "Where's Hinkleman? And is that body Mr. Coleman's? Were the Scion employees all in on this, even at the board and its leadership and management levels? In which case, *everybody* is collateral damage."

"In which case, they're more than happy for all of us to show up on the vessel," Kerrick said, sitting back and staring at Griffin. "And take us all out."

"Well, that's the problem, isn't it? We would hope not, but how can we not consider that?"

"I don't want to consider any of it. I'd like to take Amanda and Brandon away from here and find some peace and quiet."

"Me too," Griffin said. "But you and I both know the world's a much uglier place than most of the average people know about."

"True enough, and that's not very nice to consider either."

"No, but the problem is, it never seems to get any better."

"Which is why we're doing what we're doing, to bring down this ring of people. But exactly what are they doing and why? Holding political prisoners for political favors or for ransom? Or holding these victims for body parts or for human trafficking? Or first to sell them off and then to harvest them once their buyer is done with them? For whatever reason they're being kidnapped and held in a prison environment. Plus research is involved, the kind of research that involves ordering body parts. … What's the chance those kidnapped people were kept strictly for body parts?" he asked with a frown. "Not about politics. Not about ransom money. Totally about body parts."

"No clue," Griffin said. "But damn I don't like that thought."

"We needed a small team for this job initially, but, at the same time, a part of me says we need some analysts to go through the company."

"The cyberteam is on it. So far they haven't found anything."

Kerrick wandered around the small room, restless. He

should be sleeping, but finally he decided that he needed to disengage his brain. "I'm catching twenty," he said as he kicked off his shoes, climbed onto the top bunk, and stretched out. After years of experience, he knew exactly how hard it was to go to sleep anywhere at any time, but he had perfected a lot of skills to help him get to the top of his game.

Within two minutes, he had his eyes closed and had already drifted into a deep sleep.

# CHAPTER 14

SHE WOKE UP when a hand gently shook her shoulder. Amanda stared up at Kerrick and whispered, her throat hoarse and her voice raspy, "Hey. What's up?" Her hands automatically stroked the side of his face.

"We'll be leaving in a couple hours," he whispered gently. "Sorry to wake you but thought you might want to freshen up before we eat. Food will be here soon."

Her brain still foggy, she attempted to focus on what was going on. And then it all came rushing back. She rolled over to her back and groaned lightly. "Seriously?"

He nodded. "Seriously."

She realized Brandon was no longer beside her and sat upright. "Where is he?"

"With Griffin. Brandon wanted to see a little bit before we left."

"Is that wise?"

"It's about 2:30 a.m. Less crew members are needed at this time. Plus, this ship is not in enemy waters. Griffin knows the deal, but he figured this would help take Brandon's mind off his father. Besides, this graveyard shift has a crew meeting happening on one of the upper floors. So ... even less seamen about."

"Still ..."

Kerrick sat on the bench beside her. He reached up and

stroked her face. "We all have to leave in a couple hours."

She yawned gently and tilted her head into his hand. "Okay. But I wish we could stay here. At least long enough to recover."

"I don't," Kerrick said with a chuckle. "I'd rather be back at a motel or an apartment."

"I thought you loved being out on the ocean."

"I do," he said. "There's nowhere I'd rather be, except for the fact that we've got hundreds of people around us." And, at those words, in a surprising move, he leaned over until their faces were almost touching, nose tip to nose tip. Then he whispered, "And it would be awfully nice if we were alone." He leaned over a little bit more and kissed her gently.

What was supposed to be just a brush of his lips was an instant melding of the two of them. He pressed hard, kissing her deep and long. Still half asleep, she woke up fast, but she also woke up every other body part of Kerrick's as she wrapped her arms around his neck and held him close. When he finally pulled free, he whispered, "Hold that thought."

"WHY?" SHE ASKED. "It doesn't sound like we'll have any privacy or be alone anytime soon."

"Not necessarily," he whispered as he leaned over and kissed her again.

Her heart quickened once more.

"We have an hour at least." Then Kerrick said, backing off slightly, "Or we can make it happen when this nightmare is over."

She took a deep breath, trying to slow her heart rate and

to calm down her racing hormones. She never did one-night stands, so this constant reaction to him had to be from her long-term abstinence added to the adrenaline-filled situation. But she didn't want to let him go. She couldn't see ever wanting to, … but what if he disappeared from her life when this nightmare was over? Her instincts said, *Grab the moment while you can.* Slowly she let her hand drift down his arm until her fingers clenched his. "An hour?"

He nodded. "Can you be quiet?" He got up, locked the door and returned so he was lying alongside her, his breath warm against her neck.

"No." Yet her head was nodding.

"Can you try?" He chuckled softly.

"Maybe."

He noted the change in her voice and smiled. "I like the thought of an hour alone with you."

"*Mmm,*" she murmured, closing her eyes and shifting slightly as his breath washed across her cheek and ear. Shivers whispered down her spine. His fingers slipped under her T-shirt, stroking across her ribs and down her flat belly. She sucked in her breath.

"Problems?"

"No," she gasped, "just sensitive."

He nuzzled her ear and, with that same warm breath driving her crazy, whispered, "Good. Sensitive works for me."

She'd have chuckled, but just then he slipped a finger inside her waistband, and it came out as a moan instead.

He took the lobe of her ear into his mouth and suckled as his fingers delved deeper under her panties. The double onslaught sent her senses soaring. Those damnable fingers. … She arched her back and twisted slightly, but he held her still, his fingers sliding deeper and deeper. She couldn't stand it, pushed up against him, mewling in need.

"Easy," he whispered.

"Not possible," she gasped, shuddering as he ratcheted up his devilish fingers. "So damn close."

"Good," he murmured. "It's great for stress release."

Her short laugh turned to a groan as her body exploded like minifireworks and ran throughout her body. Her nerves, already sensitive, sent shudders through her body.

He held her close, gently stroking up and down her body. "Perfect," he murmured. "So sweet."

"For me, yes," she whispered as her body slowed down, leaving her replete and toasty warm inside and out. "But not for you."

"We still have time."

She burst out laughing. "Oh, so that's your nefarious plan. I'm hardly likely to argue now."

"You weren't arguing a few moments ago either," he said, his gaze twinkling.

"So true," she readily admitted, snaking her arms around his neck and pulling him on top of her. "Not now either."

"Except for this next part, where we're both wearing too many clothes." He rolled off her and, within minutes, was down to his skin. He eyed her clothing, then, with typical military efficiency, had her stripped down to the buff just as fast. She lay here and let him work, amazed at the speed with which he got things done. With their clothes dumped on the floor, she opened her arms and whispered, "I'm so ready for round two."

His gaze heated up, and he came down beside her. "Good," he whispered, "as I find I can't wait anymore."

With their fingers linked, he raised her arms overhead

and slid down her body, suckling, licking, … kissing …

Her senses, already simmering, flashed with heat once again. She gasped at the sensations surging through her, the fire licking at her nerve endings. "Kerrick," she demanded, "I want you with me this time."

His breath rasped heavily in reaction, but he worked his way back up before claiming her lips once again. She widened her thighs, wrapping her legs around his hips and urging him closer. When he accepted the offer, the emotions that overtook her were too much; … she turned her head away as he simply entered her, her body suddenly liquid, molten fire pouring through her. Simply his touch, his arms tight about her, his breath featherlight on her neck, the warmth of his body, the ultimate physical joining …

Just when she thought she couldn't take any more, he started to move. Deeper and deeper he drove in a slow and steady tempo, until he gasped and broke the rhythm to drive harder and faster, until he ground his pelvis tighter against her. Even his somewhat muted guttural cry, an erotic sound of his own completion, sent her over the edge right after him.

HE CUDDLED HER close, his body satiated and replete. In more ways than one. He couldn't remember sharing this sense of joy, this heartwarming closeness before. She was so damn special, and he had no intention of losing her when this mission was over. That they had a long way to go to get to the end of this nightmare would just give him more time to cement this beginning.

His job itself was problematic but not an insurmountable one. Besides, Amanda would likely be so driven in her work that he'd be the one making adjustments along that way more than she would. He smiled at the thought. He'd be okay with that. He admired the work she was doing. And understood her passion. That was important. When one followed their heart, it would take them where they needed to go.

That's what he'd done, and he couldn't stop anyone else from following their own heart. As long as she was willing to share her heart with him too.

# CHAPTER 15

AMANDA WOKE TO warm kisses at her neck. She curled toward Kerrick only to hear his muted laughter. "Sorry, sweetheart, not this time."

"We're leaving?" She opened her eyes and smothered a yawn.

"Soon. We used up all that spare time." He kissed her nose. "And we'll have company soon." He shifted off the bunk and dressed quickly.

"Is it safe to leave the ship, you think?"

"I'm not sure," he said. "But you haven't been totally safe so far, and you're still doing better than when you were in that prison."

She gave a clipped nod. "Good point."

She swung her legs over and sat up on the bunk. "I guess no showers, huh?"

"No time," he said. "You can have a quick wash, and then Griffin'll be back with Brandon. We'll eat some food and leave right away."

She nodded, scooped up her discarded clothing, and made her way to the bathroom. After using the facilities, she indulged in a quick wash, then did the best she could with her hair, but it was well past the point of doing very much. Still, when she stepped back into the main part of the room, she found Brandon, holding up toast topped with something.

"Didn't realize the food was here already," she exclaimed, studying the makeshift table, the food and … "Coffee," she exclaimed a little too loudly, clapping a hand over her grin.

Kerrick smiled at her as he held out a cup. "I gave you a few more minutes in the bathroom."

She nodded and accepted the coffee from him. "I didn't even think there would be much in the way of food here."

"Special circumstances," he said.

At that, she studied his face, frowned, and said, "Nobody on board knows we're here, do they?"

She caught Griffin's gaze, and he shook his head. "No, they don't. And we'll keep it that way."

She nodded slowly and took several sips of her coffee. She eyed the breakfast options, everything from muffins to breakfast sandwiches. Brandon ate eggs on toast. She picked up a muffin and quickly unwrapped it and ate it, even as Kerrick handed her a breakfast sandwich. Then, with both of those down, and the rest of her coffee too, the tray was polished off. Soon came a subtle knock on the door. Kerrick immediately stood, walked the tray over, handed it out, and said to the others, "It's time to go."

He ushered them out one at a time, Brandon still chewing the last bite of his food, whereas Amanda busily wiped her hands off as she followed them out single file. There was no sign of anybody except for their special host. They were led through another maze and into an enclosed narrow circular ladder, where they climbed and kept climbing and then kept climbing some more. If she had been claustrophobic, their small room would have done her in, but here, for sure, she would have not handled it well.

When they were at the top of the flight of stairs, the hatch was opened, and they were let outside to find themselves on a huge deck. The wind gusted at them, but very early morning gray clouds reigned. They were atop the ship now, nearing a helicopter pad—with a helicopter ready to go, its engine running and its rotors cutting into the air, awaiting them. Crouching down, they quickly raced over to the side of the chopper, where they were lifted into place.

Brandon exclaimed in joy. "Wow, a helicopter and we were just on one of those great big warships!" He kept bouncing from seat to seat, trying all four behind the chopper pilot. Amanda immediately sat down closest to the window and out of the way. Brandon took the opposite seat, and Griffin sat beside him. With Kerrick beside her, they were buckled in, each given a headset, and the helicopter lifted off.

She noticed several large black bags were to one side. *Probably Griffin's and Kerrick's gear.* She wished it were clothes for her, but all she had were the black clothes she had been given to wear for this trip. She was thankful for these. Her old ones were gone. She also dreamed of a good shower followed by a long soak in a hot bath with bubbles and fresh clean clothes of her own, but that wasn't to be. Not yet. She stared out the window.

"You okay?" Kerrick asked through their headset.

She smiled and nodded.

"Ever been on a helicopter before?"

"A couple times."

Brandon heard her and leaned forward to stare at her in awe. She just grinned at him and said, "Enjoy. They're fun."

At that point in time, Brandon peppered Griffin with question after question after question. But Griffin was patient and calm as he answered as many as he could. She wondered if he could keep it up the whole way, but, after about twenty minutes, it seemed like everything overwhelmed Brandon, and he sank back into his seat and watched in silence.

She didn't know how long they would be gone or how far they would travel, but, at this point in time, this was all about trust. And she had placed her trust in Kerrick right from the first time they'd met. It wouldn't change anytime soon.

Kerrick laced his fingers with hers. She squeezed his fingers and smiled.

"All right?" he asked.

"I was just thinking about how much my life has changed since somebody threw a hood over my head," she said, half joking.

"Any idea who it was?"

"No," she said, "not really. But I remember Hinkleman wasn't at work that Friday before the Sunday I was taken. Granted, he didn't work weekends, but I always did. And he knew it. So he must have informed the kidnappers, and they just waited until I left the building, because I didn't keep to any schedule. Meanwhile, Hinkleman was probably already at that old sanitorium, that prison, waiting for me to arrive."

"It's quite possible," he said. "Hopefully we can bring this to an end soon."

"I still don't understand what the research ship is supposed to tell us."

"Hopefully everything," he said cheerfully. "At least if we're lucky."

"Good," she said, "but it's still a little disturbing."

"Of course it is," he said. "But we'll get the answers we

need from the people on that ship."

It took them several more hours, where they traveled by helicopter to another naval ship; then they were switched out to another helicopter aboard that ship and finally landed at a small port off the Norwegian coast, where they were thereafter put into the smaller ship and taken out to open waters. Brandon continued to find the experience amazing, whereas Amanda had gone quiet. She never argued or questioned. She just followed.

Kerrick was amazed at the amount of trust she had put in him. He mentioned it once, and she shrugged and said, "In for a penny, in for a pound apparently."

He squeezed her hand, realizing he kept physical contact with her the whole way, even at one point in time wrapping an arm around her shoulders and tucking her up close. Now they sat on a small bench behind a table in this last ship. "This is the final stop."

She nodded. "We've already slept and ate our way through this set of travels. What is it that you want us to do when we get to the research ship?"

"That'll be a little tricky. Chances are, you'll stay on this vessel."

"Why?" she asked in surprise.

He nodded at Brandon, who had crashed once again. "I don't want him there."

"So why bring us here at all?"

"Because we couldn't leave you behind," Griffin answered from the seat across from her. "We thought about leaving you with various people, but we didn't want to take the chance that it would be the wrong person."

She frowned and then gave a clipped nod. "That makes sense, so thank you for that. But I still think we should all get on the research ship together."

"Have you been on it before?"

"Yes," she said, "I have. For other conferences. As part of one of my degrees, I spent several weeks out on this particular ship."

"Good," Kerrick said. "What can you tell us about the layout?"

There followed a discussion of the different levels of the ship, the way the cabins were laid out, where the labs were, where the computer centers were, and where the pilot's center was. Kerrick was fascinated by the insights she provided. "This should be very helpful," he said.

She nodded. "I hope so."

Just as they finished up, the pilot called down and said, "We're two nautical miles away."

KERRICK HOPPED UP to take a look at the research ship up ahead. "And we're delivering for them, correct?"

The ship captain nodded. "A bunch of supplies they were supposed to take but were missed. So, good timing on your part."

And suddenly they arrived at the side of the ship. Immediately Kerrick went on board and became one of the two men helping to unload the parcels and the packages, the foodstuffs, and the computer gear. He helped carry everything up the ladder and onto the vessel. If these supplies had been loaded while the ship was still docked, heavy equipment would have been used.

But, while the ship was at sea, it all had to be hand lifted, some with the use of a winch. And as soon as he found the opportunity, Kerrick disappeared into the bowels of the research ship. He knew Griffin would take the same opportunity. He tapped his comm twice to let Griffin know he was safely on board. Kerrick knew the pilot would take his place to help unload.

He quickly moved to the far side of the research vessel, keeping to the blueprints he carried in his head, as he raced toward the engine room. He was doing a full sweep, checking to see how much security and what kind of manpower they had on board. After he cleared the bottom level and moved up, he found the sleeping cabins. Some were opened; some were closed, and some were locked. But, so far, he saw nothing suspicious.

It looked like a good fifty people or so were on board. There was a galley and a full kitchen, in which they had five or six kitchen and housekeeping staff. The vessel was not fully loaded as far as hired help. But then it was a research ship, not a cruise ship. Neither was it a private yacht.

He kept out of sight and, when he had an opportunity, snagged one of the uniform shirts from a supply closet and put it on over his regular clothes. It was a rough fit, but it would work. It would allow him to move a little more publicly. He kept going through floor after floor. Meanwhile, Griffin, after he cleared each floor, gave back a clear signal. Finally Kerrick stepped up on one of the upper levels where the big conference rooms were, with all the glass windows overlooking the water.

He heard voices in the background and a speaker. Part of the conference was ongoing. So far, he hadn't seen anything suspicious as to what the hell was going on and how this was connected. He went back down a level, which was just above water level and had open decks. He walked through, looking like he had a purpose. A few people worked behind the fully stocked bar. He headed for the more internal lab room.

Just then Griffin tapped his comm—but only once. Kerrick tapped back once and got the same answer—that meant to warn him something was off. He disappeared quickly down the hallway and headed for the labs. It was a big area that he had yet to check out. As he neared it, inside the lab, he could hear two men arguing.

"What the hell are you doing here?" one asked.

There was silence and then a hard smack.

In his heart, Kerrick wondered if Griffin had been caught.

Instead, a whiny voice answered, "You know I have a reason for being here."

"Nobody comes on board without our approval first," came the first voice and then an audible sneer. "And that doesn't include you."

"Hey, you know I'm valuable. I'm the one who gets you all the stuff you need," the whiny voice said.

*Mr. Coleman*, Kerrick guessed.

"Sure, and still you asked for more money and tried to blackmail us," the first voice snapped. "Research is important. We're trying to save the world. Remember?"

"Dr. Hinkleman, I'm trying to help you" came the whiny voice.

"And what about your son?"

*Bingo. Mr. Coleman.*

"What about him? I told you that he didn't matter."

"And yet, we had to hold him, to control him, when you couldn't."

"I know," his father said. "So let me be useful again. Let me help you fulfill some of these orders. You know you have these special requests. If you need to keep my son a bit longer, then keep him. Otherwise, send him home, so he is not your responsibility."

"Your son blackmailed us," the man snapped.

"He's a kid. He didn't know what he was doing."

Kerrick froze and wondered at that. Was it really possible that Brandon had blackmailed Hinkleman? *Absolutely.* Brandon was smart enough. And maybe he hadn't realized what the consequences could be, and maybe he was trying to help his dad or trying to get his dad to stop doing what he was doing. Is that really why Brandon had been kidnapped? It would be interesting to get Brandon's take on that. It's not like he'd proffered any of this information earlier. But Kerrick felt the boy got an unexpected education from the evil side of the real world this week. Poor kid.

"The kid's not important," his father said. "You need to let me help you guys. You know I have the ability to do more."

There was silence. The other man appeared to consider it. "I'll talk to a couple people," he said. "But the fact that your son was privy to such sensitive data and then blackmailed us makes us very leery about the security of your operation and your accounting system."

"He's just one of those genius kids," the father said. "Look. I'll take care of it."

"Meaning, you'll take care of Brandon?"

"If … I … have to," the whiny voice said. Now there was a sullenness to it.

"His brain would be interesting to study," the other man said.

Mr. Coleman sucked in a loud breath.

And then the other man laughed and said, "See? You

don't really intend on silencing your son."

"There's got to be another way without killing him," the father said. "I'll send him away so he never comes back again. He won't know anything now."

"Which is why we're keeping him," the same voice said with a snarl.

"Still doesn't change the fact I can get you what you need," he said.

"I said," the man screamed, "I'd think about it!"

Then shuffling sounds were heard, and suddenly the door to the lab room opened, and a man was shoved out into the hall. The door was slammed hard in his face. The man, a small one, a weasel with haunted eyes, caught sight of Kerrick and sneered. "What do you want?"

Kerrick crossed his arms over his chest and said, "I guess it depends if you wish to see Brandon alive or not anymore." He caught the flash of fear in Mr. Coleman's eyes and realized Brandon's father really did care.

"And with one call, you are done," the father snapped.

"Says the guy who sells body parts," Kerrick said slowly.

He nodded. "Yes, I do. But they're necessary for research, and, all over the world, medical research is important."

"But maybe you supply them a little too fresh, don't you?"

The weasel stiffened in front of him. "You don't know anything about it." And he stormed off down the hallway.

Kerrick wasn't sure if he should let Mr. Coleman go or not, but it had been an interesting conversation. It confirmed Brandon's father was alive, so that crispy critter in the morgue had the wrong name on his toe tag. It also confirmed that the father still cared about his son. What would he do if he knew that his son was close by?

Kerrick hoped the boat-for-hire had pulled off far enough away that Brandon and Amanda weren't being questioned. On that note, he turned the knob on the door beside him and pushed. It opened easily under his hand. He stepped inside to see somebody in a white lab coat sitting between a computer and several unknown specimens near a microscope. None were identifiable. Not to him anyway.

The man turned, looked at him, and glared. "Not just anybody is allowed in here. Get out."

"I have something you need."

"And what's that?" he sneered.

*Your punishment.* "And, of course, you have the one thing I want."

Confused, the man straightened and walked closer. The name on his white lab coat read Hinkleman.

Kerrick gave a feral grin. Exactly who he'd hoped to find.

"What is it that you want? Not that I give a shit."

"What is it? I have questions, and you should have answers. That's all that there is to know," Kerrick said as he reached behind him and locked the door.

The man studied him, saw the movement, and frowned. "I'll call security."

"Go ahead. But, before they get in here, you'll answer a few questions, like why you had your cohort Amanda Berg kidnapped and imprisoned."

"Oh, you overheard that conversation, didn't you?" He sneered. "Well, I don't expect you to be smart enough to understand, but she was a problem. We take care of our problems."

"And how many problems are you taking care of?"

"Who cares? People always want somebody to take care of problems. I just happened to be in a position where I had a problem of my own that I could take care of at the same time."

"So, do you kidnap all your victims for your research purposes?"

"God, no," he said. "Although a tempting proposition. But, if it ever got found out that we were using humans for live trials without approval and then killing them when our research fails and selling their body parts ..." He shuddered. "Just the paperwork alone is a disgusting thought."

Kerrick knew all this confessing by Hinkleman would be safeguarded by Kerrick's ultimate death on board this ship. *Not today, Doc.* Kerrick decided to take advantage of the doc's willingness to share by asking more questions. "So, what were you doing with Amanda? Would you kill her eventually or just keep her imprisoned for life?"

"Well, if her damn research had worked, I would have killed her," he said. "But the fact is, it doesn't work, so I need her."

"Too bad she escaped then, isn't it?"

At that, Hinkleman froze. "You shouldn't be here." He stared at him and asked, "Who are you?"

Kerrick smiled and said, "One of the men who helped rescue her." The words were barely out his mouth when he lunged for the doctor, his fingers going around his throat and the back of his neck. He hit a pressure point, and the doctor opened his mouth to scream, but only a half gasp came out, and he sank to his knees.

Kerrick kept up the pressure until the doctor fell face-forward to the hard floor, knocked out. Kerrick quickly took the lab coat off Hinkleman, tied him up with zip ties—he never left home without them—and dragged his captive around to the back of the labs. He found a closet that would barely hold him.

Then, with Hinkleman's lab jacket replacing the uniform shirt that he wore, Kerrick quickly went through the information sitting on the computers. He sent a message to Griffin and to his Mavericks cyberteam. He got a response back from the chat people that made him smile. But he had no time to deal with that.

He studied the monitors full of information. *Interesting.* Hinkleman had ledgers and correspondences opened. There were letters with Norway addresses. So Hinkleman was doing business there as well. Kerrick quickly downloaded the material and sent it off to the US government, the UK government, the French government, and the Norwegian government. Somebody needed to know what the hell had been going on. With all the computers up and running, and with information flowing as fast as the internet signal could carry it, he heard a sound outside in the hallway. He tapped his comm to see if it was Griffin, but Kerrick got no answer. He tapped again and got no answer. *Shit.*

Suddenly the door opened, and Griffin stumbled in, falling to his knees, where he was then kicked to the ground. The two men behind Griffin pointed their handguns at Kerrick. "You, get away from the computers."

Kerrick stood and slowly stepped to the side, acting like he belonged here. "Of course. What's the problem?"

And somebody else came from behind the two gunmen and shoved Brandon to the floor beside Griffin. Amanda was then pushed inside as well by a few more people—none of those armed as far as Kerrick could see.

More people filed in the room, pushing everyone else

forward. Looked like the conference-goers had gone vigilante.

She looked up at Kerrick, each walking slowly to the other, and smiled sadly. "It was the pilot from the ship."

He swore softly.

She nodded. "Everybody's into betrayal these days." The look on Amanda's face was pitiful. She whispered, "I'm sorry."

He gave a tiny shake of his head and reached out a hand. She placed her hand in his, and he yanked her beside him, just narrowly avoiding Amanda being knocked to the ground by one of the gunmen. "Wow, what a big man you are. Beating up a woman and a child."

The group of men standing in front of him just jeered. "We knew you were coming. You know that, right? We were ready for you."

"Hardly," he said calmly. "Is this the geek brigade? A bunch of desk jockeys with guns in their hands for the first time? Where is the real security team?" He glanced at the computers, all the screens showing signs that his transmissions were in progress but hadn't yet been completed. As he looked, so did they.

"What did you do?" The closest gunman, the one with the curly hair and glasses, raced to the computers and quickly tapped on its keys.

Kerrick just shrugged and said, "Figured your information needed to be shared with the world."

The gunman turned and belted Kerrick across the face.

His head snapped to the side, and he let his body turn in the same direction. As he flipped around, using the force of the blow to drive him along, he heaved a healthy right cross, making contact with the gunman's jaw. He must have had one of those weak jaws because he went down with a slump.

In an instant, more guns were raised in Kerrick's direction. He looked at the gunmen insolently and said, "Who'll sign your paychecks now?"

Frowning, a man in the back stepped forward. "You can't stop our paychecks."

"Good," he said, "more proof of what you've done. Because all the data found here on this ship, documenting all your illegal acts, is right now going out into the ether and spreading far and wide to various countries' governments, so they all know what you've been up to."

"*We're* not up to anything," the man in front sneered. "What do you know? You're a pirate trying to take over our ship."

Kerrick laughed. "Is that what you think we are? Is that what the *good* Dr. Hinkleman told you? Do you want to know what Hinkleman's really been up to? He's been kidnapping people and holding them prisoner, taking money from other people to make certain individuals disappear, who then become body parts, special-ordered organs." His gaze was hard and glassy.

The man in front frowned. "I don't know what you're talking about. We're here for a conference. If we had realized we would come up against pirates in this area, trying to steal our research, we would have brought in more security. But as it is …"

"As it is, you have a lot of security—where is the real security detail, by the way?—considering this is deemed a medical or scientific conference," Kerrick said. "You can't be so naive as to think this company and the scientists here are do-gooders, can you?"

One of the men standing off to the side, another white-lab-coat wearer, protested, "We are do-gooders. We're trying to cure some of the deadliest diseases."

"Only with very unorthodox methods and purchased by blackmail money, right?"

He had the grace to look shamefaced. "I don't know what you're talking about with the body parts that are special ordered, but we had to raise additional money somehow. Hence the new facility."

"Where you kidnap people and keep them as prisoners?" Amanda cried out in shock, pointing to Brandon. "He was taken, and he's a ten-year-old boy."

At that, even more confusion crossed that speaker's face. He looked down at the boy and back up at her, then frowned. "Well, he wasn't a prisoner. And what do you mean by *prisoners*? These were people who needed special care. We had to develop a special sanitarium with very high-end solutions, and these people were very grateful."

"Absolutely. I know *I* was *very* grateful," Amanda said, almost screaming in frustration. "Don't you realize what's being done to those people? They're held in a comatose state. I know because I was held in that prison. I got a tray of shitty food full of drugs once a day, if I was lucky, with one flimsy blanket and nothing but a chamber pot and a floor. That's all we had for facilities and cleanliness! And this child endured the same treatment."

The man just stared at her in shock. "No, no, no. We created and built a very high-end sanitarium for people who have extraspecial problems and require extraspecial medical attention, where the families don't want anybody to know."

"Have you ever visited the facility? I suggest you do. And the families too would be interested in seeing that."

"You mean, the families pay you to keep these people

drugged out of their minds and away from their fortunes?" Kerrick asked.

The scientists all looked at him in shock.

"No."

"Not possible."

"Certainly not."

"Yes," Amanda snapped. "Just like you're stealing these people's lives, Hinkleman wanted my research to call his own."

"Your research?" Several of the scientists turned to look at her.

She nodded. "I'm Dr. Amanda Berg. I work at and am a major shareholder of Scion Labs, but, gee, I wasn't invited to this meeting, was I?"

"We heard you were dead."

"From Hinkleman, I suppose?" she growled. "I was kidnapped on the way from work. Thrown into the back of a lorry and drugged for a day so they could transport me from Paris to that London sanitarium and then inject me with a tracking device without my knowledge. When I woke up, I was a prisoner in a cold concrete cell with no windows and only a thin blanket on a rickety cot and a tray of drugged food once a day.

"Hinkleman visited me twice. He walked in and told me that my data was corrupt. He was so furious that he couldn't read my research notes that he smashed my face with his fist and walked off. I suspected that, after another day or two, he would have been chaining me to my computer chair to fix my data," she snapped. "Instead, I escaped and found this little boy in another prison cell and got him out of there too."

"Dr. Hinkleman said he had a breakthrough," one of the

men in the back shouted.

"Of course he did," Amanda said wearily. "He's that kind of guy, isn't he? Makes everybody else do all the work, and, when they find a breakthrough, he steals their work, takes the credit." She shook her head. "The animal trials were complete. I needed to move on to the human phase, but my results have been excellent."

"So, how do you explain that your data is corrupt?"

She gave him a half smile. "I often work in a partial shorthand style for my own use. It's faster, and I've been doing so much research that I know exactly what I'm talking about. But Hinkleman hadn't even looked at my research at that point. Until one of my coworkers told Hinkleman that my cure was working. So he had me kidnapped so he could steal my work, so he could be known as curing cancer. Yet he's too stupid to decipher my notes."

A hard rumble of conversations began before them.

"How many of you are a part of Hinkleman's research team? Here at this conference?" Kerrick asked the maybe one dozen men who crowded around the doorway or had stepped inside the room.

"Twenty-five of us are from Scion," one of the men said. "We came because we expected to hear an excellent announcement from the company."

She nodded. "Likely about the success of my cancer cure research."

"And some of us purchase items via Scion," said the other man who'd been horrified to hear about the prison firsthand. "I need a certain amount of pancreatic tissue for the type of work I'm doing, and I get that through the company."

"Of course you do," she said, "but you can also get it

from other companies. The boy's father is the one who supplies Scion with organs and tissue, and it can be a very dodgy business. We're hoping to determine if the body parts he's been dealing in are hand selected by someone *other* than the donor."

The men's faces expressed shock and dismay and absolute horror.

"And why can't you go through established biomedical companies?" Kerrick asked. "Many people donate their bodies to science. You could certainly get a tremendous amount of pancreatic tissue that way."

"But I needed it fresh," the man explained. "Within hours of curating it. And preferably not preserved with the chemicals that are usually administered."

"So, when Hinkleman gets one, is it airlifted to you?"

He nodded. "Absolutely."

"And how many do you order?"

He shrugged. "A couple a week maybe?"

She nodded again. "It'd be interesting to see where they came from. Don't you agree?"

His face paled. "I sure hope you're not implying that he killed people to bring me pancreatic tissue," he said, his voice faint. "That goes against everything I believe in."

Kerrick spoke up. "All we need is a tissue sample from all your Scion purchases, and a DNA match can be run. I'm guessing all your donors have been murdered."

A collective round of gasps could be heard about the room.

"And you each paid Scion Labs to attend this conference?" Kerrick continued.

"Yes, we all do. Even the employees at Scion, I understand, pay a conference fee as usual," the pancreatic customer stated. "Scion Labs puts it on every year, but this year they said they had some great announcements for customers and employees alike, so we should all attend. Plus, they had new supply lines of various products that are needed by us and others. And we can only get through the company."

"Such as the pancreatic tissue?" Kerrick asked.

He and several other men nodded.

"I need adrenal glands," one said. "And that's just part of it. We need fresh tissue samples in order to accurately determine the effects of our testing."

"You don't know what it's like trying to get the permissions to do human trials," one of the men said. "The red tape is notorious. And we're all applying, but, in the meantime, we're working on a limited amount of testing material."

"So you've expanded into working on human volunteers? People who are past the point of being cured, so that you have some test data?" Kerrick asked.

He shrugged.

"Willing volunteers who have nothing to lose and have lost all hope otherwise? But the sample size is still too small, right?" Kerrick asked.

"What most of you need to understand, both employees and customers, is that the Scion Labs itself has become diseased," Amanda said. "Yes, I'm a majority shareholder, but Hinkleman, who is the chairman of the board, has been leading Scion Labs down an ugly path."

"It still doesn't explain why all these people have been kidnapped and imprisoned, and yet, haven't been killed and harvested for body parts already," Griffin said, straightening up in front of her.

"I think it's for blackmail money, another source of steady income to add to the funds collected through the fake sanitorium project," she said. "I think it's pure and simple all about money, power, and greed. Because someone has to fund all this research. You who are customers of Scion all have received grant monies from the company, didn't you? That's why, when they called, you jumped?"

At once, many of the men looked around to the group and then said, "Yes. That's exactly right."

Amanda nodded. "I presume an audit of the company will find that an accurate accounting will not cover all the grants given out to customers, like those gathered here today. Hinkleman was working many angles here, even both sides against the middle—like kidnapping people for blackmail money, to hand out as grants to customers, who then buy body parts from Hinkleman, which he freshly provides from people he's murdered, all while charging you to attend conferences such as this one. I believe Hinkleman may even be surgically removing the organs at the sanitarium where I was jailed. We will set out to prove that as well."

The sounds coming from their audience grew louder.

Amanda turned to Kerrick. "Where is Hinkleman?"

"He's got a bit of a headache," Kerrick said with a grin.

"Can he answer questions?"

"Maybe," he said to Amanda, "but we need to make sure we have everybody rounded up, so nobody is left to cause trouble when we aren't looking." Turning to the crowd, he asked, "Where is the real security team?"

"And sharing all we know with all gathered here today," Amanda said.

Kerrick grinned. *Inciting a riot … directed at Hinkleman.* He liked how this woman thought.

Several gunshots were fired into the air behind the collection of men gathered in the lab. Several cries of alarm followed as everyone turned to face a new threat. Brandon clutched Griffin's waist and stood behind him, while

Amanda was tight against Kerrick, his arm wrapped around her shoulders.

She whispered, "You were right. I should have figured Hinkleman had more security around here somewhere."

Kerrick glanced around, moving her farther behind him. A large refrigerator-freezer cooler was off to the side, to hold working samples, Kerrick imagined. He glanced at it, wondering if she could be safe from gunfire inside it.

She firmly shook her head and said, "Not a chance." However, a letter opener was off to the side of a nearby table. She quickly grabbed it and slipped it up her sleeve.

He grinned. He admired her quick wit. Although he had two weapons on him, it wasn't the right time to show his hand. He needed a distraction first. Seems Amanda was preparing for that.

As the scientists were urged to crowd in closer, four more gunmen stepped forward, their faces grim as they surveyed the group.

"We were hoping to not have to do this," one of the men said.

"Head of security, I presume?" Kerrick asked.

He shrugged. "And a shareholder in the company."

"If I had kept my mouth shut," Amanda said cheerfully, "you wouldn't be in the position of having to kill all these scientists and researchers now, would you?"

He glared at her. But the gasps from the people around them rose in horror.

"There's no need to kill anybody," another security guard said in a soothing tone. "Nobody here will talk. They're all involved."

At that, there was a dead silence. Yes, the scientists, the researchers, the customers, the employees would all soon realize just how much their *involvement* now meant.

# CHAPTER 16

AMANDA WATCHED AS the group was quickly separated. Scientists, Kerrick, Griffin, Brandon and herself were off to the other side. She hoped that Hinkleman's security team would at least let a child live. But she wasn't so sure. She heard a pounding on the door behind her. She glanced over when the head security gunman motioned at one of his men to open the door.

Hinkleman struggled to get out, blood flowing from an injury to his temple. He tried to remain steady on his feet, but he was clearly woozy. "Shoot them," he screamed uncontrollably. "Shoot them dead." He spun toward the head of security. "Drayden, you promised me that you'd take care of everyone. Shoot them, damn it."

*Drayden?* Something was familiar about the large man's bearded face. She frowned. "Were you the one who kidnapped me off the street?"

He sneered at her. "No."

"Are you sure?" she insisted. "You look very familiar."

"It wasn't him," Hinkleman cried out, almost dancing in place. "It was his brother, Haron. He worked on your father's secret security detail." And he laughed as though crazed. "You were so easy."

Shocked, she had the puzzle pieces falling in place now. "No wonder we never could get in touch with Father's security detail to figure out why they lost track of me. Because they were silenced or were part of my kidnapping," she cried out in outrage.

Just then another man stepped forward, who she hadn't seen yet in the background. His features were immediately recognizable. "Haron, I presume?"

He grinned. "Absolutely."

"Why?" She shook her head, dazed. "Why would you be a part of this?"

"For the oldest reason in the world," he said in a smug tone. "Money."

"And my ex? Is he a part of this?"

An odd light lit up Haron's gaze as he glanced over at Hinkleman. "That was Father's idea."

*Father?* Stunned, she spun to Hinkleman. The shocks just wouldn't quit. "You had your sons kidnap me?" she asked him, but little sanity remained in that gaze. She pivoted back to Haron. "What role did my ex play in my imprisonment?"

He laughed. "Not much but the one meal and one bottle of water a day was his request …"

"That slimy little bastard! It's been five years. What's his beef with me now?"

"Something about how that's all you left him with—enough money for one meal a day."

"But he won't get even that now, will he?" Kerrick asked shrewdly, an arm tucked around Amanda. She curled in closer.

The smile disappeared from Haron's face. "What do you know about it?"

"Well, if you took out the three delivery guys from the Dover side of the ferry, I highly doubt you planned to leave

Amanda's ex-husband alive to talk either. Once you charged him as much money as you could get from him—and it wouldn't have been much, I imagine—then you took him out."

"It's none of your business," Drayden said. "That's enough talking."

"Not quite," Amanda snapped, turning to Hinkleman. "What about those other people you imprisoned? What were you doing with them?"

Hinkleman glared at her at first. Yet, when he finally spoke, his tone was placating, as if talking to a child. "I can hardly let them go, can I? They are a great source of income, month after month after month. Rich people will pay an incredible amount of money to remove a *problem*."

"Like Cynthia and Peter?" Brandon shouted. "They didn't want to be there any more than I did."

"Kids *may* be seen but *not* heard," Drayden snapped.

"It's all right, Brandon," Kerrick said. "A full sweep was carried out, and they've been found. They are in a proper hospital, getting treated even now."

Amanda looked at Kerrick, catching his smile, and felt her heart lighten as he explained, "I only heard a few minutes ago. I just hadn't had a chance to tell you."

"Well, I'm glad to hear that."

"It doesn't matter," Hinkleman snapped. "We'll start again."

"Not from prison, you won't," Amanda stated.

He stopped, stared at her, and said, "You can't stop me. Besides, how did you get here?"

"They were in the boat that came with the supplies," the head of security said. "We told you when we left port that nothing else was to get on board exactly because of shit like this happening." He motioned in disgust at Kerrick and Griffin.

Hinkleman saw Kerrick and pointed a finger at him. "That man attacked me," he roared. "Shoot him right now."

Seeing the confused yet horrified looks on all the scientists' faces as they witnessed this unfolding drama meant more and more of them were now Team Amanda, abandoning Team Hinkleman like a sinking ship. Kerrick grinned at Hinkleman. "What's the matter, Doc? Everybody now knows that you're behind all this nastiness. That you're getting paid by families to keep certain relatives, who they don't want to deal with, in a drugged-out state in a fake sanitarium that is really a jail cell. That you're keeping a little boy prisoner so his father continues to remain silent and will still provide all those lovely special-order body parts that you want at low prices and at speedy time frames.

"But here's some further bad news for you. I only heard about it five minutes after I stepped inside this lab. Did you know that the rest of the board wants to remove you as the chairman? That they want to open a full and complete investigation into your dealings?"

Spittle formed at the doctor's lips. His face turned bloodred, and his hands were fisted and shaking with rage. He turned to the head of security and reached for his rifle, but the gunman lifted it up and out of his way. "No killing, Dad. That's up to us."

"You kill him right now!" Hinkleman screamed, his voice dead hard, his eyes wild. "I don't want to see that man take one more step."

Kerrick smiled, took two steps toward Hinkleman, and watched him back away, his eyes wide and afraid.

"Is what he said true, Hinkleman?" asked one of the scientists. "Did you get us all involved in something so despicable?"

Hinkleman stood up straight, gathering his courage again maybe. "You had no problems getting involved. All you cared about was getting your grant money. Well, we gave you the grant money," he sneered. "So, you owe us, and *we own you.*"

Then he turned, stared at his son, the head of security, and pointed at Kerrick, saying, "And I trust that that man does not get off this boat alive."

As Hinkleman took several steps past the head of security, Amanda called out, "If he doesn't get out alive, I'll publish my research under my own name while you rot in jail—that is, if you make it off this ship alive."

Hinkleman turned, stared at her with an ugly twisted expression, and said, "What is he, your lover? I'm sure these gunmen will take care of you, so you won't need him further. That's all you're good for anyway. Goddamn females."

Amanda laughed, making him angrier. "What you really mean is, isn't it too bad that a *woman* found the cancer cure, which you've been looking for after all these decades. You didn't even have the brainpower to figure out my research notes." Her tone bordered on insolence, hoping to push him over the edge. She'd seen it happen once before, and it was a scary sight. But she needed him to lose it right now because it was the diversion they needed.

"You're old. Washed-up," she taunted. "Never did have the brains for this. Just another strutting rooster. *Useless.*" Then she added the coup de grâce. "No wonder the board wants to get rid of you."

He stared at her as a scream of pure rage let loose from

his mouth. "Shut up! Shut up!" Spittle flew from his mouth as he backed up a step, his head shaking, as if incapable of seeing anything but her.

Definitely, he did not see reason.

"No, Dad, stop!"

But he was beyond hearing anyone.

He screamed a second time, but this was a cry of that evil rage from deep inside him as he raced toward her. "Bitch! Stupid cunt! You don't know anything!"

Drayden tried to grab his father to hold him back, but Hinkleman launched himself into the air, his fingers out like claws.

Amanda stepped to the side as he stumbled to the ground. Then she kicked him as hard as she could in the temple. He didn't move. She turned and looked at the curly-haired gunman, still pointing his weapon at her, and asked, "Really? Even now, hearing all we've said, this is the kind of man you choose to work for?"

Curly shrugged. "A paycheck's a paycheck."

"So nobody in your family has died of cancer or lost a breast because of breast cancer?" she asked gently. Curly stiffened. Her gaze zeroed in on him. She nodded. "That's the research I'm doing. I've turned a corner on perfecting my cure, and this guy wanted to steal it from me. He's the true pirate here. And yet, he can't even read my notes. He's not smart enough to do the science. Is that what you want to stand for?"

He stared at her, trying not to reveal his thoughts.

Then Drayden, Hinkelman's son and the head of security, said, "It doesn't matter if anybody in his family has cancer or not. They'll probably be dead before your medicine gets out there."

"Maybe," she said. "I mean, after all, Hinkleman kept me as a prisoner for days, with barely enough food to stay alive and only one bottle of water a day. Hard for me to work on a cure in that condition."

More of the gunmen frowned, and she nodded. "Yeah, didn't you know that was the evil you were working for? That people like me, the brains in this world, are being drugged, yet who were trying to find answers, but who stood in Hinkleman's way of getting his name declared as the one who found the cure for cancer or the next big breakthrough. Then there's the boy, … and those of us who didn't even know that we were crossing a line, and yet, we got thrown in Hinkleman's fake sanitorium, which is nothing but a prison."

"I don't know anything about kids," Curly said defiant-ly.

"Well, you're hearing about it right now," she said. "Hinkleman had his goons kidnap Brandon here," she motioned to where he stood watching the scenario intently, "a ten-year-old boy and locked him up all alone in a cell with little food and water and a chamber pot and a cot with one threadbare blanket *for nine days*. Just like they did to me, but I only had to endure a couple days in his jail. You know why? Fear is a great carrot to force people to do something they wouldn't want to do. I can't even imagine how many other people they've done this to before killing them.

"Of course some misguided family members or plain evil people are paying Hinkleman to hide away problem family members, while some people Hinkleman has targeted to be kidnapped simply because their family is rich or because Hinkleman wants fresher body parts."

She sauntered closer to where the good doctor lay unconscious on the floor and gave him a shove with her foot. "If you've got a spare bullet, you should put it in his head. He's the lunatic mastermind behind all this shit. Just what the world needs. Another guy who takes money to lock up innocent people and then to throw away the key. Who has people killed for money. Who has people kidnapped when his supply of illegal body parts runs low."

She reached down, but the gunman said, "Don't touch him."

She straightened and looked at Curly. "Or what?"

He immediately lowered the rifle and pointed it at her chest.

She smiled and walked right up to the rifle until it touched her. "Then pull the trigger, and you can kiss that cancer cure goodbye."

Curly stared at her, his gaze hard. "My mother," he said, "she died of breast cancer."

"And she probably carried the gene too," she said gently. "I'm sorry for that, but, if any other females were born into your family, they're in trouble too."

He swallowed and jerked his head. "My daughter."

"I can't help her in here," she said. "I can't guarantee to cure her, but we're getting incredible results now. That's why Hinkleman put all this together and locked me up, so that he could steal my research and be the king of the cancer cure."

Curly stared at her, undecided.

She shrugged. "Your choice." Then she turned and walked over to Drayden. "So now what? This is your game now that the doctor, your nutty father, is out of commission. It's all about you and your brother now." She couldn't believe all the people who had lost their lives for their mistake in becoming involved with this group. And for what? Just money? That seems to be all Jimmy, Stanley, and Tom got out of it.

Drayden sneered. "He's my father, not my boss, you know? We were willing to work with him when the money was flowing, but he's always been difficult. Now …" He shrugged.

She smiled and nodded. "Good thing because now you'll have to figure out exactly what you'll do with all of us. I presume about fifty people are on board this ship, counting everybody, whether working or drinking or sleeping?"

He nodded.

"It'll look very suspicious when everybody aboard this one ship shows up dead or missing."

"I'm just here for security purposes, to keep everybody in line and to make sure it's going well. This was our father's show."

"So, are you letting us go or not?"

In response, he lifted the rifle and pointed at her. "Not."

"Okay," she said in that determined voice of hers. She turned her back on him.

*BALLSY MOVE*, THOUGHT Kerrick. *Might be time for some gunplay.*

When she looked at Kerrick, she held up three fingers against her shirt, then immediately put one down.

He raised his eyebrows.

When she put down another finger, he sent a subtle hand signal to Griffin.

When her final finger was lowered, three people moved in concert: her, Kerrick, and Griffin.

All found their targets.

She stepped to the side of her gunman, pivoted, pulled the letter opener from her sleeve, and stabbed Drayden in the throat. Haran cried out as his brother collapsed.

Meanwhile Griffin took out one of the two civilian gunmen with one chop to the throat, while Kerrick did the same to Curly.

And, just like that, Amanda held a machine gun herself, facing off the rest of the real security team, as did Kerrick and Griffin, but from behind.

She coolly took stock of the other gunmen and asked, "So, what'll it be? A bloodbath or will you lay down your weapons?"

The three remaining security officers, looking down the steady aim of her machine gun, turned just enough to see Kerrick and Griffin behind them. Armed too. They all stared at her in shock, slowly lowering their weapons to the floor.

Kerrick looked at her over the security team caught in the middle and said, "What the hell …?"

"My father taught me to stand up to bullies." She smiled. "You're welcome."

"If you ever pull a stunt like that again …" he snarled, but then he and Griffin knocked out the last of the gunmen. Kerrick stood, hands on hips, shaking his head, his stare locked on Amanda.

She walked up, kissed Kerrick gently on the lips, and said, "Or what?"

A high-pitched giggle came from behind the group of scientists who'd been holding Brandon back during the chaos. Released Brandon raced toward them and launched himself in the air. She held out her weapon to Kerrick, who snagged it from her hand. Then, she grabbed Brandon, picked him up, swinging him around.

He held on tight. Just then another voice cried out, "Not so fast."

She turned to see a scrawny old man in the doorway, tentatively holding a gun. "Not again …"

Brandon looked at him and cried out, "Dad!" He ripped himself free of Amanda's arms and raced over to the man.

The man stared as his son raced toward him, shock on his face. "Brandon?" He threw down his weapon, opened his arms, and crushed Brandon tightly against his chest.

It brought tears to Amanda's eyes to see how well-loved Brandon truly was.

His father had tears dripping down his face as he raised his head from embracing Brandon to look at her. "I don't know what the hell happened," he said, "but thank you for bringing my son here."

"You're welcome," she said with a smile.

Kerrick spoke up, saying, "She rescued him from Hinkleman's prison."

The older man, his throat working hard as he held his boy tightly, nodded and said, "And I'm damn glad to see him. Even after kidnapping my boy, then setting fire to our home, to my place of work, I did everything I could—from groveling to blackmail to get my son back—but they weren't having anything to do with it."

"That's because I'm special," Brandon said, pulling back and looking up at his father. "But she's special too."

His father looked over at her and said, "Special?"

Brandon smiled. "She's just like me."

Brandon's father reached out a hand and said, "My name is Willie, and you have my ever-grateful thanks."

She eagerly shook his hand. "You're welcome. He talked

to me in Morse code," she said with a big smile. "Not sure how many people in the world can do that."

"He's been talking in Morse code since he was a toddler," Willie said. "The fact that you even understood him is a miracle."

She turned and introduced Kerrick and Griffin. "And these are the men who rescued both of us."

"We obviously have a lot of answers and information to share with each other," Willie said to Amanda. "Why don't we all gather in the boardroom?

"Griffin and I'll get these guys secured and stowed away, and we'll join you."

"That works for me," she said, watching Kerrick, who already had four of the six gunmen tied up and secured. She smiled at the others gathered in the lab and asked, "Shall we discuss science, or shall we discuss the future of the company, or shall we discuss both?"

"How many shares do you hold in the company?" asked one of them.

"I'm a thirty percent shareholder," she said gently. "There could be a corporate takeover happening after this fallout settles."

A lot of nods and murmurs of agreement followed as Willie ushered everyone else from the room, staying behind with Kerrick, Griffin, Brandon, and Amanda.

Kerrick laughed. "I can see you doing that too. Are you sure you want to run a boardroom?"

She gave him a horrified look. "Hell no. Absolutely no way. But I'd love to get back to my lab. Somebody else gets to run the company, not me." She looked over at him with a cheesy smile on her lips. "Come on. How about you?"

"The only weapons I like in my hand," he said, "are rifles. Or handguns. But never a pen."

"I'm not so sure about that," she said. "I did some research on my own, and you've got an MBA in business." She didn't mention the loss of his wife and daughter. They had time to discuss that in the years to come.

He shrugged. "Still don't like a boardroom. I'll take a shoot-out any day."

"We'll see," she said with a smile. "As long as you stay close, I don't mind."

"But what if somebody else needs my help way across the world?"

She nodded. "Then you go. But you have to promise me that you'll always come back."

He gave her a special smile and whispered, "I can make that happen."

Brandon followed the exchange like a tennis game, then turned to look at Amanda, then at Kerrick, and back at Amanda. His gaze landed on Griffin, and he said, "See? I told you."

Griffin laughed. "You did, indeed."

Brandon held out his hand. "You owe me."

Griffin pulled his wallet from his pocket, selected a five-dollar bill, and said, "You will make a great con man someday."

"No con about it," he said as he tucked his winnings in his pocket. "You just gotta have the smarts." He tapped his head and smiled, turning back to his dad. "I told you that you should get rid of these guys."

His father nodded. "Well, maybe now that we have a new major shareholder in the company to deal with, we can make some big changes."

And, with that, they all trooped to the boardroom.

But Kerrick grabbed Amanda by the hand and pulled her back. She spun so fast that she found herself in his arms, pressed against his chest. He looked down at her and whispered, "Meaning?"

She looked up at him, her eyes soft and gentle. "You've been in the cold for so long, I think it's time that you found a way home."

"And where's home?" His tone was brisk, but she could see the vulnerability in his eyes.

She grabbed his hand and placed it over her breast. "Home is here. In my heart." She nodded gently and whispered, "I knew as soon as I met you. That's the problem with being smart. Sometimes I know things before others do."

A slow smile stretched across his lips as something dawned in his eyes. He whispered, "No. I knew as soon as I saw your photo." He gently tapped her lips. "I was hooked." He leaned over and kissed her gently, once, twice, and then she wrapped her arms around him and kissed him hungrily.

She whispered, "I'll admit defeat as long as you stay with me."

"Forever?"

"Forever," she affirmed, reaching up and kissing him again, their bodies locked together, heart, mind, and soul. It wasn't just him who had come in from the cold. So had she.

# EPILOGUE

GRIFFIN WOKE TO an odd buzzing on his night table. He glanced at the clock—2:03 a.m.—then around at his surroundings. Still in the same hotel room stateside that he had been living out of for the last week. Like Kerrick, Griffin was at a crossroads. He needed a real home but had no idea where it should be. If he continued to work with the Mavericks, he could live any damn place. They'd fly him to his op. He had some ideas but …

His phone's insistent buzz brought him to full awareness. He grabbed it and frowned. "What?" he answered.

"Your services are needed," said the stoic voice on the other end.

"Again? So soon?"

"What can I say? The world's a mess," the voice said.

"Not sure if I want to do any more of these specialized jobs," he said quietly.

"Understood, but you have a unique skill set."

"And what's that?"

The other end went quiet.

Griffin wiped the sleep from his eyes. "Am I going in alone?"

"You can choose one. You'll have all the support you need in the background as usual. And, if you need more backup, you only have to ask."

"What about Kerrick?"

The voice hesitated. "How about Asher or Jax?"

"Jax? Jax Darrum?"

"Yes."

"I didn't realize he was part of the team."

"We're considering it."

Griffin laughed. "Meaning, he hasn't said yes, and you're hoping that, if you can get me to work a job with him, it'll be a yes."

"Potentially." There was a dry sense of humor in that voice. "Kerrick is around, but he'll run communications on this one."

"You mean, that mysterious chat window?"

A slightly muffled cough could have easily been a chuckle when the voice said, "And maybe a little more."

Griffin frowned. "What's the job?"

"You're heading out in the USS *Anzio*."

"Wait," Griffin said. "I'm not going anywhere until I hear what the job is."

A loud sigh traveled between the phones. "The daughter of a British media newspaper mogul has been kidnapped and is being held in Thailand."

"And what's stopping the military from going in and grabbing her?"

"We only have one garbled message, saying that she's married now and that she belongs with them."

"And what does she say?" he asked, frowning. "Since when did a marriage keep somebody prisoner?"

"In many countries, it does keep them a prisoner, which is why she couldn't get the word out to us that she's being held."

"How long has she been detained?"

"Three days."

At that, Griffin straightened up in bed and threw off his blanket. "Three days? And you knew about it all this time?"

"No, we only got intel that this was a possible kidnapping at midnight. We've been waiting to get confirmation."

"Well, I have to get there fast then," he said. "That won't be a couple hours' trip."

"True," the voice said. "We can fly you partway, but we don't want you entering the country using any passports."

He swore. "So my face isn't to be anywhere?"

"No, hence the ship."

"Sure, but going from California to Southeast Asia? That's hardly a twenty-four-hour event."

"True enough. But, as you'll see, there are other ways to go from one place to another. Be by the docks at 0600 sharp."

And, just like that, the voice rang off. Swearing silently, Griffin realized he had less than four hours to be there. He got up, quickly packed, then showered and dressed. He would need food, depending on what was going on with his transportation. He looked over at the Chinese food he'd had last night and shrugged. "Cold Chinese food. Yum. I've had worse." He used food as a sustenance and an energy source, hence keeping a selection of protein bars in his ready bag.

But still, it wouldn't be enough. Depending on what was happening on board ship—and whether he was there officially or secretly—he could or could not be fed. He quickly finished off the chow mein, tossed the empty containers, and stepped out of his hotel room.

He had called for a cab, but instead the vehicle that pulled up was black and military-issued. He stepped into the passenger side and looked at the driver, surprised to see Jax.

"Wow," he said. "They did convince you after all."

Jax shot him a hard look. "A one-time deal," he said. "And only because I know you're the one going out on this op."

"Not alone if you're coming with me," Griffin said, returning his friend's hard look with one of his own. He knew Jax from several overseas missions. He was a good man to have in your corner but an even better one if it entailed night work. "Apparently, we're supposed to get in and out without anyone knowing we were there," Griffin said.

Jax shrugged his shoulders. "So what else is new?"

They parked as close to the wharf as they could. Each picked up their duffel bag and tossed it over one shoulder. Then the two men walked to the end of the docks. A Zodiac waited for them. The pilot looked up at them, nodded toward the back, and said, "Let's go. We're late."

Shrugging at that, both men hopped into the Zodiac, and it took off without any fanfare. By the time they reached the cruiser, they were led to the top deck. And still, without anybody saying a word, they were taken to a separate room, a small sleeping area. With shades of Kerrick's mission in his mind, Griffin walked in the claustrophobic room, dumped his duffel bag, and planted his hands on his hips as he stared around. "Do you know anything more about this than I do?"

"I know Jax shit," Jax said with a grin at the play on his name.

"Well, I don't know anything either," Griffin said, his tone harsh.

Just then a single rap came at the door, and a red envelope was slid underneath. Griffin quickly opened the door, hoping to see who had delivered the letter, but nobody was in the hallway. Like this was some ghost ship. He snatched up the envelope and tore it open. Travel instructions.

"Interesting," he said. "We're supposed to be in Thailand by noon tomorrow. *Thailand time.*"

"So we're flying parts of it then," Jax said.

"Yeah, but I already checked. Any commercial flight takes nineteen to twenty-five hours. We better be flying Air Force One to make Thailand by then. Right off the bat, we're short like fourteen hours, just because of the time differences. Could be more like fifteen hours ahead, depending on which part of Thailand we're dealing with."

Jax groaned, then threw himself on the top bunk. "I didn't get much shut-eye last night."

"Who did?" Griffin muttered. Trouble was, he was hungry again. The leftover Chinese food hadn't done the job. He quickly pulled out his phone to check if he had any internet. He did, since they were still in port. He sent off a message. *Envelope received. Travel instructions received. No damn food. No coffee.*

He put away his phone and dropped to the bottom bunk, an arm across his eyes. It was one thing to be part of a well-oiled Navy SEAL team on board a ship. They did constant training when they went out to sea. Everybody had orders; everybody had instructions, and everybody had a part to play. In this scenario though, Griffin didn't know what part he was supposed to play. That had been the same problem for Kerrick. After all those years of disciplined navy life, Griffin found the freedom something to adjust to. But he'd do just fine.

Helping out Kerrick had been a hell of a way to drop into this Mavericks system. Griffin wasn't even sure it's what he wanted to do long-term. He'd been on the fence when he'd been tagged to help out Kerrick—who was going in alone—and, well, that wasn't Griffin's kind of a play. Nobody should go into these shitstorms alone.

And, if some woman had been kidnapped, … well, two men would have good chances of survival and success where they might need more than just backup. His phone buzzed, and an encrypted file popped up with a note. His eyebrows shot up at that. He quickly followed instructions to decode it and went through the file on Amelia Rose.

"That's the daughter we're supposed to find," he said, raising his phone to flash her picture to Jax. "Except it's beyond dated."

"Is she really being held against her will?" Jax asked. "That's one of the biggest issues here. Was it her who put out the cry for help, or was it somebody else?"

Griffin was still going through her file when he froze, looked at the date, and swore. "I'll say it wasn't her choice," Griffin snapped, studying the data in front of him.

"And how do you know that?" Jax said.

"She's eleven years old."

Jax peered over his top bunk at his partner on the bottom bunk, and said, "What the hell?"

Griffin nodded with a grimace. "She's just a child. It says here she was kidnapped, along with her nurse and her tutor."

"And how old's the nanny? If she's gray-haired and sixty, we're in trouble."

"The nurse is sixty-eight. So, yeah, we're in trouble. The tutor, however, is thirty-two and speaks three languages. Her name is Lorelei. Lorelei James."

"So Lorelei got the word out?" Jax asked curiously.

"Most likely," he said. "But, as usual, our intel is very skimpy."

"It seems like we go into these jobs with less and less

intel each time," Jax said. He waited a moment and then said, "I heard a few details about your job with Kerrick, but it went okay, didn't it?"

Griffin groaned. "It did, but it was touch-and-go a couple times. That kid, Brandon, he was something else."

"Didn't Kerrick say something about the woman he rescued being part of the same high-IQ group?"

"Yes, she's back in her lab. The entire corporate organization has been reshuffled as she stepped up in power after all the changes. Her father had also stepped up and bought a whole pile of shares and handed over voting power to her to give her complete control of the company."

"Wow," Jax said. "Not bad for her. And I guess Kerrick is sticking around Paris."

"Yeah, and he's running communications for us this time."

"What the hell does that mean?" Jax asked.

"I think it's the Mavericks command center. Nobody is allowed to know what we do, where we're from, or what our histories are."

"So, are fake IDs in that envelope for us?"

"Maybe," he said, "but I didn't think so." He grabbed the red envelope, opened it again, and then whistled gently. "Well, there is now. They were stuck to the inside of the envelope." He quickly ripped off the tape, releasing the IDs. He handed one to Jax. "This is you, *Malcolm*."

"Whoever invented these names," Jax said, "should be shot."

"Hey, it's way more normal than your real one," Griffin said with a laugh.

"You're one to talk," Jax said. "Who names their kid after some legendary creature in Greek mythology?"

"I think Griffins are found in many different societies back then," he said. "So, whatever. It's unusual enough, but I've always liked it."

"I like mine too. But can't say much about *Malcolm*."

"Well, that's all right in my opinion," Griffin said, groaning. "I've been renamed as *George*."

At that, Jax chuckled. "That sounds lovely."

"It makes me sound beyond old. It's supposedly an unassuming name. I'm George Harris," he said. This time he checked the inside of the envelope more thoroughly—to the point where he ripped it open. "Okay, I don't see anything else in here. But this is a journalist's media pass, and, if you look on the back, it's got a British citizen's ID card."

"As if we look like Brits," Jax said with a scoff. "And I certainly don't have an English accent."

"I don't think you need to worry about that," he said. "I think it's a case of nobody gets to look at these close enough to double-check."

Just then another single knock came. Both men hopped up, with Jax standing behind the door. Griffin suddenly opened the door, hoping to surprise whoever was on the other side. But, once again, no one was there. There were, however, two large trays of covered food. He looked at it and smiled. "Well, at least my text did something."

"What? Did you text, asking for food?" Jax said, chuckling.

"Hey, if we've got a lot of traveling to do, I want to make sure I'm fed. I cannot do anything if I don't have energy."

"Oh, I agree with you. I'm just surprised you got service so fast."

"One thing I learned from that last op with Kerrick," he

said, "is that anything, *absolutely anything you want*, you just ask for it. They do their best to deliver."

"Good to know."

They brought the trays inside, sat down, and stared at the covered dishes. "It's still cafeteria food though, isn't it, just under a fancy domed plate?" Jax asked.

"But a step above," Griffin said. "I don't know about you, but I got steak and prawns."

Jax looked over at Griffin's plate in shock and said, "Seriously?" And then he lifted a different lid and said, "Look at that. I do too."

"But you don't like prawns, do you?"

"No. I'll trade you for your steak."

"Hell no," Griffin said. "I'll just eat your prawns when you're done with your steak. I know you won't eat them, so I don't have to give you anything." He gave Jax a big grin. "Good deal for me."

With that, the two men quickly polished off their meals, and then, even though it was early in the morning, they stretched out, and this time both crashed.

This concludes Book 1 of The Mavericks: Kerrick.

Read about Griffin: The Mavericks, Book 2

# The Mavericks: Griffin (Book #2)

What happens when the very men—trained to make the hard decisions—come up against the rules and regulations that hold them back from doing what needs to be done? They either stay and work within the constraints given to them or they walk away. Only now, for a select few, they have another option:

The Mavericks. A covert black ops team that steps up and break all the rules … but gets the job done.

Welcome to a new military romance series by *USA Today* best-selling author Dale Mayer. A series where you meet new friends in this raw and compelling look at the men who keep us safe every day from the darkness where they operate—and live—in the shadows … until someone special helps them step into the light.

**Helping Kerrick was one thing, getting tagged for a mission of his own quite another …**

His heart ached to hear a young girl had been kidnapped while at a hotel in Thailand, waiting for her father to arrive. But nothing is ever as it seems, and this case isn't even close to simple.

Lorelai spent the last seven years enjoying her young charge, Amelia Rose. Tutoring the daughter of a wealthy business owner added perks to the job, like holidays around the world. In all these years Lorelai had never once seen the downside to having big money–until the holiday in Thailand where Amelia Rose is targeted, and they were both kidnapped.

Griffin managed to rescue the kidnapped victims, but tracing the kidnappers was a whole different story and brought the group a little too close to home …

Find book 2 here!

To find out more visit Dale Mayer's website.

https://geni.us/DMGriffinUniversal

# Author's Note

Thank you for reading Kerrick: The Mavericks, Book 1! If you enjoyed the book, please take a moment and leave a short review.

Dear reader,

I love to hear from readers, and you can contact me at my website: www.dalemayer.com or at my Facebook author page. To be informed of new releases and special offers, sign up for my newsletter or follow me on BookBub. And if you are interested in joining Dale Mayer's Reader Group, here is the Facebook sign up page.
http://geni.us/DaleMayerFBGroup

Cheers,
Dale Mayer

# About the Author

Dale Mayer is a *USA Today* best-selling author, best known for her SEALs military romances, her Psychic Visions series, and her Lovely Lethal Garden cozy series. Her contemporary romances are raw and full of passion and emotion (Broken But … Mending, Hathaway House series). Her thrillers will keep you guessing (Kate Morgan, By Death series), and her romantic comedies will keep you giggling (*It's a Dog's Life*, a stand-alone novella; and the Broken Protocols series, starring Charming Marvin, the cat).

Dale honors the stories that come to her—and some of them are crazy, break all the rules and cross multiple genres!

To go with her fiction, she also writes nonfiction in many different fields, with books available on résumé writing, companion gardening, and the US mortgage system. All her books are available in print and ebook format.

## Connect with Dale Mayer Online

*Dale's Website – www.dalemayer.com*
*Twitter – @DaleMayer*
*Facebook Page – geni.us/DaleMayerFBFanPage*
*Facebook Group – geni.us/DaleMayerFBGroup*
*BookBub – geni.us/DaleMayerBookbub*
*Instagram – geni.us/DaleMayerInstagram*
*Goodreads – geni.us/DaleMayerGoodreads*
*Newsletter – geni.us/DaleNews*

# Also by Dale Mayer

## Published Adult Books:

**Hathaway House**
Aaron, Book 1
Brock, Book 2
Cole, Book 3
Denton, Book 4
Elliot, Book 5
Finn, Book 6
Gregory, Book 7

**The K9 Files**
Ethan, Book 1
Pierce, Book 2
Zane, Book 3
Blaze, Book 4
Lucas, Book 5
Parker, Book 6
Carter, Book 7

**Lovely Lethal Gardens**
Arsenic in the Azaleas, Book 1
Bones in the Begonias, Book 2
Corpse in the Carnations, Book 3
Daggers in the Dahlias, Book 4
Evidence in the Echinacea, Book 5
Footprints in the Ferns, Book 6

Gun in the Gardenias, Book 7

Handcuffs in the Heather, Book 8

## Psychic Vision Series

Tuesday's Child

Hide 'n Go Seek

Maddy's Floor

Garden of Sorrow

Knock Knock…

Rare Find

Eyes to the Soul

Now You See Her

Shattered

Into the Abyss

Seeds of Malice

Eye of the Falcon

Itsy-Bitsy Spider

Unmasked

Deep Beneath

From the Ashes

Psychic Visions Books 1–3

Psychic Visions Books 4–6

Psychic Visions Books 7–9

## By Death Series

Touched by Death

Haunted by Death

Chilled by Death

By Death Books 1–3

## Broken Protocols – Romantic Comedy Series

Cat's Meow

Cat's Pajamas

Cat's Cradle
Cat's Claus
Broken Protocols 1-4

## Broken and… Mending
Skin
Scars
Scales (of Justice)
Broken but… Mending 1-3

## Glory
Genesis
Tori
Celeste
Glory Trilogy

## Biker Blues
Morgan: Biker Blues, Volume 1
Cash: Biker Blues, Volume 2

## SEALs of Honor
Mason: SEALs of Honor, Book 1
Hawk: SEALs of Honor, Book 2
Dane: SEALs of Honor, Book 3
Swede: SEALs of Honor, Book 4
Shadow: SEALs of Honor, Book 5
Cooper: SEALs of Honor, Book 6
Markus: SEALs of Honor, Book 7
Evan: SEALs of Honor, Book 8
Mason's Wish: SEALs of Honor, Book 9
Chase: SEALs of Honor, Book 10
Brett: SEALs of Honor, Book 11
Devlin: SEALs of Honor, Book 12

Easton: SEALs of Honor, Book 13
Ryder: SEALs of Honor, Book 14
Macklin: SEALs of Honor, Book 15
Corey: SEALs of Honor, Book 16
Warrick: SEALs of Honor, Book 17
Tanner: SEALs of Honor, Book 18
Jackson: SEALs of Honor, Book 19
Kanen: SEALs of Honor, Book 20
Nelson: SEALs of Honor, Book 21
Taylor: SEALs of Honor, Book 22
SEALs of Honor, Books 1–3
SEALs of Honor, Books 4–6
SEALs of Honor, Books 7–10
SEALs of Honor, Books 11–13
SEALs of Honor, Books 14–16
SEALs of Honor, Books 17–19

## Heroes for Hire

Levi's Legend: Heroes for Hire, Book 1
Stone's Surrender: Heroes for Hire, Book 2
Merk's Mistake: Heroes for Hire, Book 3
Rhodes's Reward: Heroes for Hire, Book 4
Flynn's Firecracker: Heroes for Hire, Book 5
Logan's Light: Heroes for Hire, Book 6
Harrison's Heart: Heroes for Hire, Book 7
Saul's Sweetheart: Heroes for Hire, Book 8
Dakota's Delight: Heroes for Hire, Book 9
Michael's Mercy (Part of Sleeper SEAL Series)
Tyson's Treasure: Heroes for Hire, Book 10
Jace's Jewel: Heroes for Hire, Book 11
Rory's Rose: Heroes for Hire, Book 12
Brandon's Bliss: Heroes for Hire, Book 13

Liam's Lily: Heroes for Hire, Book 14
North's Nikki: Heroes for Hire, Book 15
Anders's Angel: Heroes for Hire, Book 16
Reyes's Raina: Heroes for Hire, Book 17
Dezi's Diamond: Heroes for Hire, Book 18
Vince's Vixen: Heroes for Hire, Book 19
Ice's Icing: Heroes for Hire, Book 20
Heroes for Hire, Books 1–3
Heroes for Hire, Books 4–6
Heroes for Hire, Books 7–9
Heroes for Hire, Books 10–12
Heroes for Hire, Books 13–15

## SEALs of Steel

Badger: SEALs of Steel, Book 1
Erick: SEALs of Steel, Book 2
Cade: SEALs of Steel, Book 3
Talon: SEALs of Steel, Book 4
Laszlo: SEALs of Steel, Book 5
Geir: SEALs of Steel, Book 6
Jager: SEALs of Steel, Book 7
The Final Reveal: SEALs of Steel, Book 8
SEALs of Steel, Books 1–4
SEALs of Steel, Books 5–8
SEALs of Steel, Books 1–8

## The Mavericks

Kerrick, Book 1
Griffin, Book 2
Jax, Book 3
Beau, Book 4
Asher, Book 5
Ryker, Book 6

Miles, Book 7

Nico, Book 8

Keane, Book 9

Lennox, Book 10

Gavin, Book 11

Shane, Book 12

## Collections

Dare to Be You…

Dare to Love…

Dare to be Strong…

RomanceX3

## Standalone Novellas

It's a Dog's Life

Riana's Revenge

Second Chances

# Published Young Adult Books:

## Family Blood Ties Series

Vampire in Denial

Vampire in Distress

Vampire in Design

Vampire in Deceit

Vampire in Defiance

Vampire in Conflict

Vampire in Chaos

Vampire in Crisis

Vampire in Control

Vampire in Charge

Family Blood Ties Set 1–3

Family Blood Ties Set 1–5

Family Blood Ties Set 4–6
Family Blood Ties Set 7–9
Sian's Solution, A Family Blood Ties Series Prequel
    Novelette

## Design series
Dangerous Designs
Deadly Designs
Darkest Designs
Design Series Trilogy

## Standalone
In Cassie's Corner
Gem Stone (a Gemma Stone Mystery)
Time Thieves

# Published Non-Fiction Books:

## Career Essentials
Career Essentials: The Résumé
Career Essentials: The Cover Letter
Career Essentials: The Interview
Career Essentials: 3 in 1

www.ingramcontent.com/pod-product-compliance
Lightning Source LLC
Chambersburg PA
CBHW071508110726